ISLANDERS

ISLANDERS

PEADAR O'DONNELL

With an Introduction by ROBERT LYND

THE MERCIER PRESS
CORK AND DUBLIN

THE MERCIER PRESS, 4 Bridge Street, Cork.

24 Lower Abbey Street, Dublin 1.

© P. O'Donnell.

ISBN 0 85342 851 46

Originally published in 1927 by Jonathan Cape.
Published by The Mercier Press Ltd. in 1963.
Reprinted 1965, 1967, 1974, 1976, 1979.
This edition 1988.

Printed by Litho Press Co., Midleton, Co. Cork.

INTRODUCTION

No one has ever taken a census of the population of men, women and children invented by the novelists. Though I cannot even guess at it, I fancy the figure must be somewhere in the millions. Yet, of all these millions, probably not more than four hundred are, or ever were, alive. Even the greatest novelists often give us books in which, while some of the characters have blood in their veins, others have merely sawdust; and many characters – Sherlock Holmes for instance – that have attained a world-wide popularity, have not been created at all, but merely invented. There is no valid objection to the invention of characters: invention is the next-best thing to creation. But we experience a special pleasure, as of coming out into the light and the air, when we read a novel in which the men and women continually come to life in a turn of the head or a turn of speech. Mr. Peadar O'Donnell, to my mind, has brought a family to life in *Islanders*. He has observed men and women, and observed them imaginatively. He knows their phrases, the details of their daily existence, their exhilarations, their sorrows; and out of his knowledge he has built up a home on a Donegal island so real to us that a woman cannot feed the hens or cut a soda cake for the children without making us wish that we were there to see her. Mr. O'Donnell writes of the poor folk of the island without either kailyard sentimentality or the realist's over-emphasis of dismal things. He is content to place Mrs. Doogan and her brood of children before us as living human beings in the circumstances of their daily life. He does this in such a fashion that the very economy of the household is interesting, and the purchase of a bag of flour becomes an important event for us as it is for them.

Islanders would be worth reading merely as a description of the lives of the poor on a wild, barren and beautiful coast, on which two bucketfuls of winkles may be a considerable addition to the wealth of the home. It is also a piece of heroic literature, however, and as we read it we positively rejoice in the heroism of human beings who can force a living from the rocks and live in charity with one another among the uncharitable stones. And, besides the daily heroism of toil and endurance, we have two supremely heroic figures in Mary Doogan and her son Charlie. In self-sacrificing, ever-busy, worn-out Mary Doogan Mr. O'Donnell has added yet another to the attractive mothers of fiction. Our hearts are wrung for her when her young daughters set off to the hiring fair on the mainland and she cries out: 'This is the first scatterin' of my childer God knows if I'll ever have ye all gathered under my wing again. God alone knows!' We share her happiness as she sees Charlie win the great race at the regatta. And her death, after the pursuit of the tricky hen that laid its egg secretly away from the house, moves us with a sense of personal loss. Here Mr. O'Donnell has mingled laughter and tears, the poetry and the prose of life. How well he brings her whole character before us with her absorption in the little needs of her children, as she lies on her death-bed, and, after the Rosary has been said over her, turns and murmurs: 'Did anybody take in the eggs? That dog of Neddy's 'll get them if not.' Only a good writer could have written the description of Mary's pursuit of the hen and her death. And only a good writer could have written Mr. O'Donnell's description of Charlie's feat in crossing to the mainland in a curragh on the night of the storm in order to fetch the doctor. The delight in courage rings in the prose here and in the story of Charlie's triumph at the regatta. And with the delight in courage there is also the delight in the beauty and the awfulness of the earth and the sea. Mr. O'Donnell is as happy in the setting of his story as in the human beings whose story he tells. We live in the landscape as we do in the story of his characters.

His sense of reality enables him ultimately to fit even the dangerous and alien figure of the doctor's sister into the story without producing the ruinous effect of a too gaudy patch. I confess I felt some alarm for the story when Ruth with her disturbing love intruded into a world of which she could never be a natural inhabitant. Charlie, happily, unlike most peasants in similar situations in fiction, never exchanges his blood for sawdust.

I do not wish to over-praise *Islanders*, but I feel sure that among the novels of the season it will stand out as one of the few in which the author has created characters that convince us of their reality, in a setting that seems to be a part at once of the geography of the earth and of the world of the imagination.

Robert Lynd

ISLANDERS

TO
My Father and Mother

Daybreak spread wearily over the mountains to the east, and crept down into the misty waste. A thin breeze chilled the ebb-tide. Loose bodyless clouds released a drizzle of rain. Inniscara Island shivered in the cold-lipped Atlantic, indifferent to a dawn that was lifeless.

At the head of the strand the island boats bulked black against the white-pebbled strand. The whitewashed cottages struggled into outline.

Up in the Doogans' house there was a light. A lanthorn was shining through the blindless window. At the fire a pale-faced youth sat on a stool. From a bed in the kitchen came the light, regular breathing of a sleeping person, breaths that carried in them the promise of an easy and full awakening.

A coal rolled down the hearth and rested against the leg of the stool. The youth took up the tongs and threw the coal back into the fire. He rested the tongs against the wall, but it slipped and fell on the flag with a clatter. The regular breathing in the bed was interrupted. There was a quick movement. The curtain was put aside, and the wan, lined face of an elderly woman was turned towards the fire.

'Put out the lanthorn, Hughie,' she said, after a pause. 'The daylight's through the house.'

He turned his head to the window, yawned gently, and getting to his feet walked over to the lanthorn, and quenched it.

'No sign of her, Hughie?' the woman said.

'She's very restless all night,' he said. 'She was standing a minute ago.'

He went out and across the street towards the byre. As he drew near he heard the deep, laboured breathing of a cow. He hurried to the door and looked in. Then he ran back to the street and called in to the woman.

'Mother,' he said, 'hurry out.'

She was out of bed in a second, and dropping a red petti-coat down over her head hurried to the byre in the bare feet. A cow greeted the woman's appearance with an eager low.

'Poor suckie,' she said. 'Run, Hughie, run, waken Mary Manus,' she said, turning to the youth.

He ran out of the house, and across the fields to waken Mary Manus. The dog barked as he came running down the green, a bark full of challenge, which promptly changed to one of greeting. Hughie tapped at the window with his fingers.

'Hoigh,' he called. 'Hoigh.'

He tapped again. There was a sound inside. The window blind was swept aside, and a woman's face appeared at the window.

'The cow's calvin'; me mother wants ye.'

She nodded her head in reply and let the blind drop. He stepped back from the seeping thatch. He heard the bolt shoot back; Mary Manus came on to the street. She was a bare-footed woman of about fifty; she was wearing a red-flannel petticoat, and was tying a shawl on her head as she walked. Hughie delayed until she came to his side.

'Seo, hurry yerself,' she said, breaking into a run.

Later they carried the calf into the house, where they shut him into a corner with the barn door taken from the hinges for the purpose. In the evening Charlie would make ready a corner for him in the byre.

Mary Manus would not wait for tea, but ran lightly home in the bare feet.

CHAPTER 2

After Mary Manus left, the mother put on a pot of potatoes that had been ready washed from the night before. When they were boiled Hughie went up to the room, where there were three beds, in which ten children were packed away at night. Sally, Nellie and Sheila were in one bed. It was a low, four-post bed, raised about a foot from the floor. Sally and Nellie were fifteen and twelve respectively; Sheila was three. Hughie was sixteen. He and Charlie had a narrow bed all to themselves. It was empty now, for Charlie had not yet returned from fishing herring in the West Bay. Charlie was twenty-two; he was the second eldest. Dan, Andy, John, James and Eoin were sound asleep; Dan, Andy and John at one end of the bed, and James and Eion at the other. Sometimes Eoin slept at the foot of the narrow bed. In the kitchen with the mother was Nabla, who was five. She had bronchitis, and slept easier in the kitchen. Hughie told them that the cow had calved, and after a few sleepy, uncertain moments there was a rush to the kitchen. Even Sally and Nellie dressed quickly.

The mother was hurrying forward the boiling of the milk. After a cow calved, boiled milk (beastings, they called it) was a thing to arouse interest among even better-fed children than the Doogans.

The mother drove the boys back to the room to put on their clothes. Nellie, responding to Eoin's sobbing appeals, went up to help them dress. Sally buttoned on Sheila's dress. Breaking away before Sally was half through, Sheila hastened to the door to meet Charlie. The dog's bark told her he was coming. Her face was aglow amid a setting of curls, as she called the glad news that the cow had calved.

Charlie was heavy with the failure of a long, useless night's work in the West Bay. It was Sheila's excitement, not the news itself, that called up a tired smile.

'An' did the cow calve?' he humoured her.

Sheila nodded. 'We'll get beastin's,' she enthused, clapping her hands.

Charlie went on up and sat on the end of a log. He stretched out weary legs to Hughie, who pulled off his sea-boots. 'Not much scales on them,' the mother remarked.

'Not a tail I saw,' he said. He yawned loudly. Steam was now rising from his wet clothes.

The mother emptied the boiled potatoes into a long, shallow basket, and placed it across the mouth of an empty tub. The boiled milk was distributed in bowls, and the children knelt round the basket, resting the bowls among the potatoes or on the floor. They had scarcely begun to eat when the mother hurried in from the street.

'Lift yer bowls, quick,' she said. 'Sit ye round the fire,' she added, pausing for a moment with the basket of potatoes in her hands. 'Leave that tub down at the back door, Sally. Quick, now.' She hurried to the room with the basket. She was back in the kitchen when Biddy Melly entered.

Biddy was a widow of about fifty, a stoutish, comfortable woman with a fat face, and a pair of narrow, roving eyes. She pivoted her head from one side tot the other continuously, and with great ease.

'Wagga, ye didn't sleep in the mornin',' the woman of the house greeted her, benedictions having been exchanged. ''Tis, I heard Peggy's donkey rattlin' the chain on the street, an' I was afraid I left the byre door open last night. Then I saw yerself out an' in, an' I saw Mary Manus goin' home. It's the cow that calved at ye,' she said, walking down to the corner of the kitchen. 'Wagga, aye, an' a fine lump of a calf; an' a heifer calf too,' she added. 'Isn't it yerselves had the luck. An' a good colour too. An' it's not many heifer calves there was after that bull of Mickey's, an' most of them had a white back. Not a finer calf I saw this long time, bless her.' She turned back from the calf, and the pivoting head was ranging the eyes over the children with their bowls of milk, and over the fire.

'The whole crowd of them is daft lookin' for beastin's,' the mother said. 'Not a drop of tay I made for wan of them yet. They're fair leppin' out of their skins for the milk.'

'All childer's that way,' Biddy said. She waved back the bowl of boiled milk that was offered to her.

'It never agrees with me,' she explained. 'Me stomach'd be at me for a week if I touched it. 'Clare to heavens it would. Ye got no herrin' last night either,' she said, addressing Charlie.

'Not a tail.'

'Och, hoch,' she commented. 'An' will there be any boat goin' out to the port, d'ye think?' she asked after a pause.

'I'm afraid not,' Charlie said.

'I was wantin' to run out, musha,' she said. She went towards the door. 'It's mean-minded enough kind of mornin',' she commented, looking away out towards the hills. 'I'm thinkin', maybe not a boat will be goin' out now that there's no fish.'

'Then there was no fish,' Charlie assured her.

Biddy went out.

'Bolt that door,' the mother said, 'till ye get yer breakfast in peace. It's under her the trot is, always runnin' to the mainland.'

'Ye might have left them at their breakfasts,' Charlie said.

'An' is it let Biddy have the world know the way things are with us,' the mother protested. 'It's not keep it to herself poor Biddy'd do. Ye never know where she'd take the sweat to yer face with it. Come, sit ye round. An' for yer lives don't wan of ye breathe a word about what ye had in the mornin' if they ask ye at school.'

When the breakfast was over Charlie went to bed.

CHAPTER 3

The mother wakened Charlie when the children's dinner was over, and they had gone back to school. Hughie, Sally and Nellie were out gathering winkles. He came to the kitchen in the bare feet, and took down his socks off the line above the fire. He rubbed the feet between his hands to shake out the sand. The mother lifted the potatoes out of the pot, that rested at the side of the fire. She set the dish on the table with a roasted salt herring beside it.

'Sit over an' take a couple of these praties while they're hot,' she said.

'Praties, praties,' he said, getting to his feet. He went outside and washed his hands in the stream at the gable. 'People can't live for ever on praties,' he continued, coming up the floor, drying his hands under his oxters.

'They can't,' the mother agreed, her knitting-needles tinkling.

'Where's Sheila?' he asked her sharply.

''Tis I sent her to school the day. They asked that every child be sent out; the average's goin' down,' she explained.

'There'll be bigger than our Sheila runnin' wild about their own doors,' he said. 'It's daftness to send her,' he added.

'They said the average was goin' down,' the mother repeated quietly.

'When are ye expectin' to get flour?' he demanded.

'The dear knows,' she said, running a knitting-needle through her hair. 'There's only eleven eggs there yet, only eleven,' she added with a frown. 'Then there's a couple of buckets of winkles.' She laid her knitting in her lap, and took out her snuffbox. She tapped the contents into a corner, and shook out a pinch on the back of her hand. 'I don't see much hope of getting either tay or flour,' she reflected. 'There's not a penny credit. We have the roof nearly ate from over our heads as it is. The only thing they'll give now

'ud be the few shillin's to take Sally and Nellie to the hirin'
fair. An' God knows I don't like to see me wee girls go away'.
'I'll go to Scotland meself,' Charlie said, rooting through
the potatoes for one that he could eat.
'Charlie a mhic, what'd we do then? Who'd be here to do
anythin'?' the mother pleaded, speaking in alarm.
'Well, people can't live on praties day in day out,' he pro-
tested, getting to his feet.
'True a mhic, but under God what can I do?'
'Somebody'll have to do somethin',' he said, going out.
The mother sat very still, looking into the fire. She was a
very worn little woman just then, and very sad.

CHAPTER 4

When the mother got to her feet she gathered the skins, and
broken potatoes into the dish and bruised them for the
hens. Then having cleared the table she stood for a moment
with her hands resting on her hips, her eyes fixed again on
the fire. She sighed, a deep sigh, and turned to the dresser.
Pushing the plates aside she took a small paper packet
from the back of the shelf and, opening it, counted the coppers it held. Her eyes went to the eleven eggs on the dresser.
She tapped her unbroken front teeth with her thumb. She
put the coppers back. She took up the dish of hens' meat:
she threw it out in handfuls, calling the hens softly the while.
A light patter of bare feet sounded behind her. Without
turning she said: 'Come her, Hughie.'
The lad who had run over to Mary Manus came to her side.
That he was her son was evident at the first gaze. There
was the same open countenance, the same large grey eyes,
strangely filled with understanding for a boy so young. There
was eagerness now and joy in his face.
'Neddy's dog got the duck egg last night again,' she said.

'It was my fault,' he said, the joy ebbing.

The mother turned towards him, the trace of a passing smile lighting her face for a moment. Without speaking she went into the house. Hughie followed her in.

'There's ninepence in coppers there,' she said, 'an' there's eleven eggs. Ye could get the loan of an egg from Peggy to make the dozen. They're tenpence the day. That'ud be nineteen pence. Flour's elevenpence a half stone, an' a quarter of tay id be sixpence. But tay without sugar id be little use.'

'I got a lobster,' Hughie said, the glow that had been crushed out returning to his face.

'A lobster,' the mother said, almost as excited as himself.

'Aye,' he said, nodding eagerly. 'I caught him in the hole behind the black rock. I gave him to Neil Jack. He gave me sevenpence.' He opened his fist and exposed a sixpence and a penny.

'Well, glory be to God,' the mother exclaimed, 'if that doesn't beat the wee wheel. Away with ye an' get the egg from Peggy. Ye'll have threepence halfpennny left after the sugar.'

Hughie went out and over to Peggy's, his married sister's. Peggy was out, but the eggs were in a row on the dresser. He took one and hurried back home.

'Ye'll catch the boat yet over at the West Bay,' the mother said. 'Get a stone of flour, a quarter of tay, and a pound of sugar. That leaves threepence halfpenny. We'll get Charlie an ounce of tobacco. He hadn't a good smoke this week. That leaves a halfpenny.'

'That'll get snuff for yerself,' Hughie said.

'Bad cess to it for snuff,' she said. 'Sheila spilled half of the last on me. I'm run out. Maybe we'd as well get another halfpenny worth. Steal away without them seeing ye. We'll give them all a surprise at tea-time. A mhic, an' mind ye don't fall with the eggs.'

She handed him the eggs in a handkerchief. A blush suffused the boy's features. The mother noticed it.

'Well, I'll tell ye what,' she said. 'I'll put the eggs into a can, an' nobody'll know what ye have. Them that'd make fun of ye for takin' eggs to the shop id have little to do. But anyway, this is the best way, an' ye can take the tay and sugar back in the can.'

She watched him as he tripped across the green. Then she took out her snuff-box and emptied it recklessly on the back of her hand and sniffed eagerly.

CHAPTER 5

Charlie went across the sand to Manus's. He met the old man himself at the garden gate. He was mending netting-wire.

'The devil take them for hens,' Manus growled, 'it'd take me all the time fixin' after them.'

'They're only a botheration,' Charlie said.

'A botheration? They're a curse! There's a speckled rogue of a hen there an' she gets through no matter what. Believe meself she cuts the wire with her teeth, or nib, or somethin'. Oh, I'll put a halt to yer gallop if ye go near the corn again,' he threatened, scowling at the speckled hen.

'The cow calved at ye,' he continued, turning to Charlie. 'That's a blessin' where there's a lot of childer. Not a tail was got last night. Well, anyway, people'll want to get the harvest in.'

'Sheila broke the sharpenin' stone,' Charlie said. 'If yer not usin' yours, I'll leave it in on me way back.'

'Ye needn't: ye can keep it till yer finished. I'm finished, I may say. A wee start'll finish me, an' that's time enough. Susan'll get ye it: it's wrapped in a piece of old sail, an' it's stuck in under the dresser.'

Charlie's step got lighter as he drew near to Manus's. It had spring in it as he crossed the street.

Susan was alone in the kitchen when he went in. She was a year or so younger than himself. She was tall: a pile of black hair was coiled at the back of her head: her face was pale but live, glowing with life rather than touched with colour. She greeted him with a smile. Her teeth were good.

'Were ye over in Biddy's last night?' he asked her, a little eagerly.

She nodded. 'Ye had yer night for nothin' outside,' she said.

'I knew fine there was no herrin',' he said irritably. 'No smell of fish more than id be in the cow market in Dungloe. Not a thing the fowl that were seen had but fry. Any fun in Biddy's last night?'

'Deel all; we spent the night testin' eggs. Biddy was settin' a late clutch, an' somebody told her a way to know whether it's hens or roosters ye'll get from eggs. She had a sixpence on the table an' a needle hangin' from a thread over the sixpence. She had the thread round her finger. She had the egg in her other hand, an' if the needle went round in a hoop it meant a hen, an' if went up an' down straight it meant a rooster.' They both laughed.

'Where's yer mother?' he asked.

'I got her sleepin' there an' I packed her off to bed. She was up an' down to our own cow till it was late, an' then your Hughie called her. She was noddin' in the corner there till I cleared her off.'

'Be over early to Biddy's the night,' he said, lowering his voice.

There was a noise in the room.

'I want the sharpenin' stone,' he added.

She stooped to get it. He stood very close to her, and he plucked a hairpin out of her hair.

'Here, give me back that,' she said, standing up with the

sharpening stone in her hand, 'or ye'll not get this. I'm near me last as it is.'

A chair was pushed back in the room.

'Early, mind ye,' he warned her, making for the door.

She was smiling at him as he turned away.

It was late when Charlie came home from the fields. The lamp was lighted in Manus O'Donnell's. He could make out Susan at the head of the table winding a cut of yarn.

He hurried his stride across the green. She would be going a' ceilidh once she had the yarn wound.

There was no light in his home except the glow of the fire. The door was open. He heard light, joyous laughter. He sensed some unusual commotion. When he entered the mother was standing at the table, a soda cake in front of her. Is was a small cake made on a pan. She was marking it with the back of the knife. The children were sitting on the hearth, their bowls of tea in their hands, and they waited impatiently for a slice of bread, each occasionally bursting into the anticipatory laugh that had caught Charlie's ear.

'What's all this?' he asked.

The mother turned to him. There was a puzzled look that inclined more to a frown than a smile on her face. She sighed ever so slightly. This, her eldest son, never fully entered into the moods of the moment with the rest of the children. He had in some way missed contact with his nest mates. It was not so much that he was disgruntled, rather was he continuously unbending, untouched. His puzzled moodishness jarred against the lighthearted abandon of the others.

'Hughie got a lobster over at the black rock,' she told him. 'That's the second time he got one out that way,' he commented.

The mother cut the marked scone into slices and shared them round. She left Charlie's on the table. She went over and sat on a creepy on the far side of the fire. Sheila and Nabla clustered at her feet. He didn't see them gobble their bread hurriedly, and then sip at their tea with great show, glancing the while at the mother: he didn't see her break off pieces off her own slice to give to them. Hughie stooped down and pulled Sheila over to him, and he plucked Nabla's dress. She turned towards him, and he frowned his displeasure at her. Charlie drank his tea and got up. It was time to go over to Biddy's.

CHAPTER 6

Biddy Melly was a widow. She lived by herself in the snug two-roomed house her late husband had left her. Though she was on the wrong side of fifty, she was light and active, and intensely interested in all that went on. The young folk of the island used to collect at Biddy's. Young folk change their meeting-place from time to time. It used to be in Dominick Rodgers's, until Dominick's daughter, who was married in the hills, came home and gave birth to twins here. Once the cradle appears at the fireside the young folk go elsewhere. It was just then Biddy's husband died, and from the time of the wake the girls got into the habit of going a' ceilidh to Biddy to cheer her up. And the lads began to drop in next. Soon it was a recognized rendezvous.

Charlie Doogan was one of the first to get there the night after the fishing. Biddy was perched on her stool in the corner. She was grating boxty. Phil Boyle was stretched on the other side of the fire, his back leaning against the wall. He had the tongs in his hands and he was making strokes in the ashes.

'Wagga, ye were fairly layin' into the hay this evenin',' Biddy greeted him.

Charlie nodded to Phil. 'Aye, I got a hole made in it.'

'Was the policeman in with ye the day?' she asked.

'Devil a policeman I saw,' Charlie said. 'Were the police in?'

'Aye, makin' the tillage.'

'I never heard,' Charlie said. He puzzled for a moment in his half-scowling way to recall why it hadn't been mention-ed. Then he remembered the excitement over the tea. He shrugged his shoulders, as he reached for a chair.

Phil Boyle laughed. He was younger than Charlie by a few months, a typical fisherman, lanky, weather-beaten.

'I followed him meself over to Dan Rodgers'. Me father was wild with me for leavin' me work, but I knew Dan'd be a pant. He was puttin' a bottom in a creel with grass ropes, an' he's not the handiest ever handled a grass rope. In comes the policeman with meself at his heels. Dan went on chewin'; whatever the devil he be's chewing I don't know.

' "You're Dan Rodgers," says the policeman, takin' up a blue form.

' "Nobody need tell me that," says Dan.

'The policeman sat down at the table and took out his pencil. He's a new man, a young fellow, an' he was in a bit of a hurry. I suppose gettin' the same story house after house gets bothersome.

' "You're married?" the policeman says.

' "I was," says Dan.

' "An' aren't ye?"

' "Once a man's married, he's married," Dan decided.

' "But isn't yer wife livin'?"

' "She was when I saw her last," says Dan.

'The policeman was getting a bit ratty. I think he would have got angry only he kept his eye on Dan, an' there he was as serious as a judge, workin' away and chewin'.

' "When did ye see her last?" he asked. Dan lifted his

head. "I see her now," he said, noddin' out the door. The policeman wrote for a minute.

' "How much corn have ye?"

' "A handful," Dan said.

'The policeman wrote somethin'.

' "How much potatoes?"

' "A mouthful."

' "How many cows?"

' "Wan profligate." An' that was all he was asked.'

'Wan profligate,' Biddy commented. 'Where at all does he get the words?'

There was a chuckle of suppressed laughter at the door. Biddy raised her head from the grating. Three girls came in. Susie Manus was one of them. Annie Nelly and her sister were the others.

'Come ye up,' Biddy greeted them. 'Pull yer feet together there, Phil Boyle, an' let them get in their stools.'

'They can sit on me,' Phil said.

'Faith, an' a soft sate ye'd make,' Biddy said, 'with yer bones cuttin' yer skin like a cow with the crupan.'

'It's not every one can be as round as a May herrin' like yourself, Biddy,' Phil countered.

Other young folk crowded in. The men lay around on the floor, the girls sitting on creepies and chairs, and on the table. Phil Boyle took down a melodeon and began to play. Soon several couples were on the floor dancing. Charlie Doogan was feeling very happy that night when he said good night to Susan Manus at the gable of the turf-stack.

CHAPTER 7

The stone of flour gave them their breakfast for a few days. It would have lasted longer only on Sunday there was a football match, and Charlie brought some mainland people to the house. Then the family went back to the three daily meals of potatoes. And when the potatoes became scarce they took to doing without any supper, except sloak and dulsk. Sheila took to vomiting when she tried to eat either of these, and the mother borrowed a tin of Indian meal from Peggy. Sheila was now being slapped at school, because she hadn't three halfpence for a new reader. Once she came home at midday crying bitterly. She had been put into a corner by herself, and would be refused admission to the class until she bought the book. Dan wanted threepence for a geography. It was a whole fortnight before they could market eggs again, and for the fourteen eggs then they got elevenpence halfpenny. The school books were made the first call on the price of the eggs. After that a quarter stone of Indian meal was all they could buy. They had Indian cake for the breakfast and on the first morning the children were in glee over it. On the second they grumbled because there was not tea.

The mother worked hard at the knitting she got. She sat up late, and tried to have a few hours again in the morning before the children got in her way around the fire. Now and then she slept in her clothes on the hearth. She was lucky, she said, in getting good knitting, socks at halfcrown a dozen... stitches on each needle, and... rows to the heel. She made it a point to finish a pair each day. She often lost time washing clothes while the children slept, so that they would be dry for them in the morning, but she finished a dozen in eleven days, and went out with them herself to the town. She had eight miles to go, and it used up a whole day, but she had tea and sugar home with her, for she was allowed credit. She had also two dozen socks and a dozen of gloves to knit. And on top of this good luck Peggy sent them over a can of oaten meal from a new ten-stone pack they had got. As a treat they had tea for the whole family, and the children went to bed well pleased with themselves that night.

Charlie came in late after a wasted evening in the West Bay. The mother had a skilletful of oaten porridge for him, and it was to be a surprise to give him the tea after it. She told him the story of how well she got on in the village, while he supped the porridge. It hurt him to see the joy a little thing like that could bring into his folk's lives. He belittled what had happened, and crushed the mother's enthusiasm into silence. He had the tea taken before she spoke again.

'The bishop is comin' next week, an' there's not a stitch on Andy. He'll have to get a suit. There's stuff in Sweeney's an' Mary Manus'd cut it out for me, an' help me to run it up, of maybe it's a cheap wee suit I'd get. There's as much winkles now as'll get it maybe. Ye'll have to run me out to-morrow evenin'. Yerself an' Hughie could get Manus's punt.'

'I'll take ye out meself,' Charlie said. Hughie stirred in his seat. 'Unless Hughie'd like to go out, too,' he added grudgingly.

'Maybe I'd get more papers if I was out,' Hughie said. 'I'd like to see what happened to the outlaw.'

'Musha, musha,' the mother commented, 'but yer the wan for the readin'. But let him come.'

Next evening they went out. Hughie hurried off at once to get the bundle of papers the railway porter usually gave him. The winkles were sold for ninepence a bucket, and measured seven and a half buckets.

Mary Doogan had the money in her fist, when she followed Charlie up the quay on her way to Sweeney's. She was five or six paces behind him, her short steps pattering on the flags in the interval between his long strides. It was the jingle of silver on the granite made Charlie turn sharply. His eye caught a half-crown rolling on its edge. It was tinkling faintly as it raced into the sea. The mother, lips tightly closed, face as pale as death, was tottering sideways.

One hand was clutching her blouse, and one was out-stretched. He caught her as she fell.

'Mother,' he said, 'Mother,' and he shook her in his arms. Then he picked her up and ran with her towards the open door of a cottage.

'Leave her down here,' a voice ordered, and he recognized the doctor. He laid her gently on the green sward. He hurried off for the priest. He was at the door when the priest and doctor came out. The mother was now sitting in the corner by the kitchen fire.

'The very thing, a good bowl of broth,' the doctor was saying... 'no, not a thing but that. I come across it again and again... just hunger, not a thing else... always the mother.'

Charlie moved back from the door and let them pass. It was growing dark when they got back to the island. The mother went on up home, Charlie and Hughie remaining to fix up the punt.

'Tell me this, Hughie,' Charlie said, 'when did ye see me mother eatin' last?'

Hughie turned grave, questioning eyes up to Charlie. 'She can never eat praties,' he said.

Charlie stared at his brother for a moment. Then he pitched an oar abruptly from him and strolled off up the creek.

CHAPTER 8

His walk broke into a trot. A nameless, sudden danger seemed to beset him. For the first time in his life he was afraid. He walked faster. The fear kept up with him. He halted. He was in a field and he sat down on a brugh. He listened like a man startled. But the night was full of the usual island sounds only. In Fartown a woman was calling ducks. A boy was whistling in Point. Oars rattled in rowlocks at the Spink. Keadue Bar was roaring.

From within himself came an explanation of his fear. His mother: 'She can't eat praties.'

'On what had she been living? Was she dying? If she were to die!'

The way he had sulked when she told him of the knitting last night had been in his mind on and off. It troubled him on his way back from the port. How was she to know that it was his helplessness made him shy of discussing their poverty? He didn't know it himself. He recalled one day Sheila reached out eagerly for him to swing her on his shoulder, when he in a bad humour walked heedlessly past. After a few yards he had come to himself, and looked back. Sheila's face was twisted up, and the tears were trickling down her cheeks. But she made no cry. And somehow the eager way his mother had opened up the talk about the knitting had reminded him, even then, of Sheila. He was suddenly very afraid she would die. He got to his feet and hurried home. The children were crying. He heard Sheila's voice, and he heard Nabla's. He heard Hughie crooning a song to put some one to sleep. He went in. The mother was peeling potatoes, making poundies for the supper.

'I wonder did any boat go out the night?' Hughie was saying.

'Where'd be the use, an' not a sign last night?' the mother said.

'What's wrong with you, Sheila?' Charlie asked sharply.

''Tis the poor thing has a grass cut under wan of her toes, an' it's sore,' the mother explained, 'an' she's sleepy.'

'I'm hungry,' the child added.

'We'll put onions in the poundies, an' you'll get yours in a bowl,' Hughie said.

'I'd rather be at the pot,' Sheila objected.

'Ye'll be at the pot,' Charlie conceded, reaching out for her.

She left Hughie and went to him, and sat on his knee while

he examined the sore toe. Later when she was asleep he laid her to rest in the kitchen bed until the supper would be ready.

'What will you eat?' Charlie asked awkwardly, turning to the mother. She, too, was ill at ease. She feared Charlie was annoyed with her for fainting: he had been very silent on the way in.

"Tis there's a scrapin' of porridge there, an' I'll warm a sup of milk,' she said.

Charlie went outside again. The light in Biddy Melly's caught his eye, but he turned away from it. Keadue Bar was still roaring, and the sound made the island lonely. Charlie went across the sand to Neil Rodgers's. Neil was married to an aunt of Charlie's. There was a close comradeship between the two men, for they ventured much together, strong in their knowledge of the boat and in each other's seamanship and endurance. Neil was mending a lobster-pot in the kitchen. He just nodded to Charlie, and then turned to locate a vacant chair.

'Pull up that chair at the table,' he said. 'Sit ye over to the corner,' he ordered two children who were making strokes on the hearthstone with the shank of a pipe. 'Pull up the chair, man,' he ordered Charlie.

'Let the children be with their drawin's,' Charlie said sitting over by the window under the lamp. 'Yer fixin' it up again,' he commented, nodding at the lobster-pot; 'it's the devil's own tearing it got.' His speech was slow. 'It's me belief the twine wasn't the best.'

A silence fell on them as it often did in the boat. Charlie's eye wandered from the lobster-pot to the children, with their drawings on the flag. A falling brand of burning fir took his eye to the fire. A pot of porridge was boiling. It was hanging on the crane. He remembered when it was a chain was down Neil's chimney instead of a crane. He had helped to put in that crane. A crane is an improvement in a house. The freedom to make an inprovement showed that the world was not pressing too heavily on Neil's folk. Improvements could not be made in his home. Then there was the cement floor. Two years ago he had helped to put it in. He stirred in his seat.

'Any hope of us shootin' the pots at the head the morrow?' Neil did not look up, but he paused a moment before replying.

'There's a restlessness in the sea the day. There's a storm raging out somewhere; the fouls is breakin' by now.'

It was a reply Charlie could have given himself. He was uncomfortable once the question had slipped out.

'Did ye ever try mullet up at the river?' he asked.

Neil's brows were still knit together. 'I did,' he said, 'an' was caught.'

'The pocket net's across the the side of Manus's boat?'

'It is.'

'I think I'll have a shot,' Charlie decided sharply. 'They'd bag themselves fast as pollock. I left Manus's punt hangin' off the point when I came in. I'll take her.'

Neil continued his work without looking up. Charlie got to his feet. There was no further word between them until Charlie went out. He passed his aunt on the street.

'What was under him when he only stayed a minute like that?' she asked Neil.

'There is some restlessness om him,' Neil said. 'He was wonderin' would we shoot pots in the mornin' off the Point.'

'Charlie was? Is it more pots he wants torn, an' the pitch that there's in the sea? Doesn't the world see there's a storm comin'?'

Neil nodded.

'It's on him the trot was that he couldn't sit until I'd give him a mouthful of brathain,' the aunt complained, straining the milk.

Neil was silent. Once or twice he paused at his work, and

then resumed hesitatingly. Suddenly he pushed the lob-ster-pot from him, and got to his feet. He took his coat down off the nail and flung it across his arm.

'I'm goin' after that fellow,' he explained. 'I never thought of it, but maybe he took a sup in the Port.'

'Troth an' that same could be true,' his wife agreed.

Charlie was gathering up the net when Neil came to him. He got to the lee of Charlie, and there was no smell of drink off his breath.

'What is it?' Neil asked. 'Is it a dance, or what?'

'No, it's some things that's wanted in the house,' Charlie said quietly.

'An' why hell couldn't ye say that out?' Neil demanded. 'We'll take my punt,' he added, 'an' we'll try Traighailla. It's the best chance.' There were no further words passed between them until the boat stole noiselessly away from the strand.

CHAPTER 9

It was a night of bustle among the stars, where tassled shades flirted at cloud-making. The sea tossed restlessly under the pressure of a distant storm. From the south came the diffused boom of a distant bar; along the white strand floated the patter of wavelets; the highway gurgled with the sand-soaked rattle of a cart. The white strand nestled within an arched headland of walled granite. A twisted wa-ter-track, scarred into the rock by the torrents of the ages, hid a rope of twisted shadow from a shy moon.

Charlie Doogan and Neil swept in out of the haze, where moon was resting its chin on the hill-tops. Charlie waded ashore with one end of the net. Neil made an arc, drop-ping the net as he circled. He came to the strand fifty yards from Charlie, and they set to work to haul in the net. They were lucky; the vigorous splashing of fish came early, and soon there was the flash of white patches in the grey water. Working rapidly, they soon had their catch safely stored in the boat. They pushed off, and rowed over under shadow of the rocks to discuss in safety their further plans. It was Charlie who first saw two figures moving along under the skyline, near the edge of the cliff. Both saw them halt and lie down, and later they saw them creep down the water-track – two inky blotches moving along a chain of darkness. The oars had rattled when they were pushing off from the strand, and sound travelled easily along the cliffs. 'The bailiffs,' Charlie whispered, with a laugh in his throat. Neil nodded.

They launched noiseless oars and slipped off furtively as they had come. They went direct to Flavin and sold their catch of trout and mullet, the sale yielding each eleven and eightpence. They sailed back to the island, Neil steering. Charlie sat in front of the mast, the jib-sheet in his hand. He never felt the excitement of such a home-coming as this before. There was joy in the thought of the surprise he would give his mother. A blast of wind brought his mind to the weather; just a passing thought. The breeze would freshen next tide, he reflected. His mind went back to his home, and his thoughts bored through to the dreary help-lessness that the night's excitement had momentarily masked. The youth in him rebelled against the helplessness; and anyway, was he helpless? A blackness darkened the sea in front of him, a dog barked a short distance ahead. The boat's bow shot into the wind and the sails flapped. They were back at the island. He got up and lowered the sail, and Neil sculled the boat into the Caslagh. Without a sound they moored her there.

'There'll be a hubbub in the mornin', for there'll be crabs on the strand to show somebody had hauled,' Neil said with a grin.

Charlie jingled the money in his pocket. 'We were lucky,' he said, 'an' so were they,' he added, turning to go across the fields home.

The door was on the latch, and he pushed it open gently. When he reached the fireside he saw that his mother had put the curtains aside and was looking out. Charlie's being out so late had puzzled and worried her. There was no wake on the island and no dance, and nobody sick, and no card-playing.

'How much is a bag of flour?' Charlie asked.

'Sea-breeze is ten and sixpence,' she answered, sitting up suddenly. 'But what puts a question like that on yer tongue?'

He pushed the coals on the hearth together with his foot until a tongue of flame shot up. 'Me an' Neil got a haul of mullet,' he said. 'See.' He pushed the handful of silver under her eyes, and then emptied it into her palm.

'Under God, Charlie, there's a fortune here. How much's in it?'

'Eleven and eightpence,' he answered.

Her face was lit up with excitement, but she was silent. 'Ye can go to the boat in the mornin',' Charlie said, turning away, a sense of littleness falling suddenly on him. He went up to the room to bed, but the mother was still sitting and he heard the jingle of her rosary beads.

CHAPTER 10

Mary Doogan borrowed flour from Peggy that morning. It was easy to borrow then, for by evening she would be able to repay it. She told Peggy how Charlie had gone off and hauled the trout, and the way he came in and gave her the money into her fist in the bed.

The postman brought a letter for Charlie. A fish agent

wanted to know whether Charlie would fish a train of salmon nets that season.

'I'll see him when I'm out,' Charlie commented. 'What else besides four stone of flour will ye get? Better get Hughie write down all the things ye'll want me to buy.'

Hughie was busy at work when Biddy Melly came in, arriving among them in the bare feet without any warning. 'Dia annseo,' she said, when she was near the wee wall at the foot of the bed. Biddy often embarrassed neighbours coming in this way.

Mary Doogan greeted her, and she went on giving Hughie the items he was to write down. She was glad, too, that Biddy would see the little pile of silver on the window-sill. After all, there was no telling what Biddy had thought the morning the cow calved when there was no sign of the teapot on the hearth. She emptied her snuff-box on the back of her hand and invited Biddy to have a pinch. It was a biggish lot of snuff to spill out so freely. Biddy only put one finger in it. 'Me head is fair light snuffin',' she said. 'I was over there in Andy Pat's and Hannah kept me snuffin' till I near sneezed me head off.'

Mary Manus came sauntering in, knitting her stocking. 'It's new'ins to see you steppin' aroun',' Biddy commented, after greetings had been exchanged.

'I'm not as souple on me feet as yerself, Biddy. Yer gettin' younger lookin' every day comes.'

'What'd ail me?' Biddy said. 'It's a bad hen can't scrape for herself without worryin'.'

'Be what I hear ye're gettin' help with the scrapin',' Mary Manus said.

'There's people in this island, an' the heaviest of their work is puttin' out rumours,' Biddy said.

'It's a weighty rumour,' Mary Manus said.

'There's more rumours than wan goin' round then,' Biddy countered, 'an' some of them roosts under yer own thatch.'

Charlie Doogan was lacing his boots and he stooped low over his work.

'I've as sunsey a wee girl as is in the parish, God bless her,' Mary Manus avowed, 'an' a warm thatch for them comes to roost under it.'

'You've that,' Biddy agreed, 'an' a brave lump of a lad drawin' on it.'

'Well, he'll be welcome, if Susie welcomes him an' the time has come,' said the cautious Mary Manus. 'But now, about yerself,' she said, returning to the attack, 'when is it comin' off?'

'Ah, have a wit,' Biddy protested. 'I saw the postman was in with ye,' Biddy said, turning to Mary Doogan, 'an' I thought maybe it was some new news ye had, for it's none of yer wans is away.'

'Indeed no, it's none of them is away, thanks be to God, yet, anyway. Indeed, it's soon enough they'll be off. I'm busy patchin' and washin ' for Sally an' Nellie bheag these days; the hirin' fair'll soon be on us.'

''Tis, the post was tellin' me he had a letter for ye the day, an' there was a power of strange stamps on it,' Biddy persisted.

'Devil such a lot of stamps ever I saw,' Charlie said, taking a coal in the tongs to light the dottle of tobacco that was in the bottom of his pipe. 'They say there's people bes gatherin' stamps. Am thinkin' it'd be worth their while to get yon envelope. Ye never know what strange stamps like that'd be worth.'

'It must be from a long distance the letter came. I said to meself I'd run over. Maybe it's Mary's brother in Australia wrote.'

'It's me own opinion,' Charlie said, 'that me uncle'll never be heard of till he walks into the island some day. People has to lose themselves in the hills there to get any good of themselves.'

'An' it wasn't from him it was?'

'Maybe there's not a letter-box within hundreds an' hundreds miles of where he is out there,' Charlie evaded.

Biddy gave it up.

'Will ye take me in a couple of stone of bran, as ye're goin' out?' she asked. 'Call in on yer way an' I'll give ye the money. I must run now. I left a cake on the fire.'

Mary Doogan turned to Charlie. She had never heard him banter like this before. It was joy to her, this family light-heartedness fitting in so well with the little pile of silver on the window.

'A dhia Charlie, it's not right for ye makin' that craythur worry an' wonder like that. Only not a bit of meself'd tell her either,' she condoned, smiling.

'An' who was the letter from,' Mary Manus asked. 'It's over to ask ye I was comin' meself.'

'A letter about a salmon net from Flavin. It's the postman swelled her head about the stamps; devil all was on it but two halfpenny stamps.'

Mary Manus produced her snuff-box, saying it was special snuff she got out of Dungloe, and the two women sat down to knit and gossip.

Charlie went off to the Port.

CHAPTER 11

That evening Charlie was mooring the boat when Susan Manus came up throught the rocks driving the ducks before her. She waited for Charlie until he came up and they dallied for a while on their way across the bank. There was a slight awkwardness between them, for they had not been together so much of late. Phil Boyle came down from the Caslagh, and the three sat on the short, dry grass. Susan, Charlie, and Phil were often together. They had been at school together; they went to their first dance together.

They met nearly every night in Biddy Melly's and went home from there in a group, except that now and then Phil would take the near way home and Charlie would leave Susan over as far as the turf-stack. One Patrick's night a visitor to the island paid great attention to Susan. He danced with her four or five times, and tried to get sitting near her afterwards. In the morning he hung round her while she got her shawl. There were few men in the school-room at the time, for island men wait outside for their girls. The stranger took Susan's arm as she moved towards the door. On the step there Charlie was waiting, and he took the other arm. When they reached the bottom of the steps the three of them stood. Susan was struggling to disengage her arm from the stranger.

Up to then the stranger was within his rights. It was foolish of him, of course, to have imagined that a girl like Susan Manus should have been without a boy of her own, but it was permitted that he try his luck with her. Once she had declared herself, however, the island code was simple. He must go off, or the favoured one must drive him off. The man who would not attempt to enforce the girl's decision in his favour would be a thing to despise for ever. But the stranger had on a collar, and he was well-dressed. He had long hair, and it was well-oiled and brushed. He could not believe that she was serious. He was still persisting when Charlie flung him across the street.

That incident had set Charlie and Susan together and apart from the other young folk on the island. From that time it was generally accepted that they would settle down together one day in Manus's. It was then Phil Boyle took to going the near way home, and Charlie and Susan dallied longer and longer at the turf-stack.

'What time in the mornin'll we be startin'?' Phil asked Charlie. 'We won't get that boat of yours afloat unless we're on foot about five o'clock.'

'We'll have to be away with the first streak of day,' Charlie said. 'Leave it to me mother to have us up in time.'
'I hate to see youngsters goin' to the Lagan,' Susan said. 'Still, six months won't be long goin' round. Sometimes a body'd like to see what the change'd be like.'
'Don't you ever go, Susan,' Phil said, laughhing. 'D'ye mind the time I was away? I thought it was goin' to be great fun, but it was an awful ould skinflint I was hired to. He begrudged ye an hour in bed. I'll never forget the four big cows I had to milk, every wan of them had as much milk as a horse. Me hands used to be numb.'
'I'd like to see ye milkin',' Susan said. 'As much milk as a horse,' she repeated with a chuckle, and gave him a push.
'Hoigh, Susan!'
It was Mary Manus calling. Susan got to her feet with a laugh, and they helped her collect the ducks. They went over with her to Manus's, and later strolled back to Biddy Melly's together.
Charlie went home early that night, for Sally and Nellie were going to the Lagan in the morning. Susan and Phil went with him. Susan wanted to say good-bye to the girls. Sally and Nellie left her home.

CHAPTER 12

The whole Doogan family gathered round the fire when Susan and Phil went out. After the rosary the younger ones were sent off to bed. Nellie had to lie with Sheila until she fell asleep, then she came back to the kitchen.
The mother had gone through the clothing they were taking with them, darning and patching with the greatest care. She had put a pocket in the inside of a petticoat in each case, and they would carry the money there coming back. Going away, Sally was carrying the few halfpence for both.

They would divide what would be left when they would be separating in Strabane. The mother's hope was that they might get hired close together.

'Isn't it terrible that people can't all live at home till they're hardened to face the world at least,' she said, running her hand into a stocking she had darned. 'It's away to the Lagan with the childer to earn a few shillin's, then away to Scotland, an' it ends up with America. This is the first scatterin' of my childer: God knows if I'll ever have ye all gathered under me wing again. God alone knows!'

'Don't be talkin' like that,' Nellie said. 'Ye frighten me.' She clasped her hands round Charlie's knee.

'Seo, well,' the mother said, 'I won't. It's only six months, and ye'll write often. Charlie'll go the length of Fintown to meet ye comin' back.'

'Will ye, Charlie?' Nellie asked eagerly.

He nodded. Then he rested his hand on her head.

'What 'am wonderin' about is, how we'll get hired. Do they come round an' offer ye money, or do we go round sayin' how much we'll take?' Sally asked.

'Ye'll all stand together an' the farmers come round an' ask ye what ye want. Then they'll offer ye a lot less, an' they'll go away an' come back.'

'Same as the Jew that was sellin' the pictures?' Sally asked.

'Just like that for all the world. But Donal Hughie has promised he'll hire ye, an' then there's Anthon Pat goin' too. They'll do the bargainin', an' you listen.'

It was late when the mother sent them all off to bed, but she herself remained kneeling in the corner, rising now and then to put turf on the fire. In the grey of the morning she wakened them. She had their breakfast ready when they were dressed.

Smoke was rising from many houses, and soon children's voices calling could be heard from the bank. Mary Doogan gave Charlie the Holy Water to shake on them all, and she stood by the gable herself until the boat disappeared round the Point.

CHAPTER 13

It was nearly a week before there was a letter from the girls. They were hired within a few miles from each other, and would meet on alternate Sundays at Mass. In Sally's letter was a postal order for two shillings that was over after their journey. That still left them with one-and-sixpence each, she said.

It was only a month later that Doogan's cow died. She took sick of a sudden. Mary noticed her restless at bedtime, and went out twice during the night to see her. In the morning she refused to get up. Phil Boyle and Charlie lifted her, and pushed her out of the byre into the garden. Mary Manus made the cure for the cow-sickness for her, and Mary Doogan went out with the post-boat to get an office.

That evening she died. They buried her up in the bog.

That very evening Mary Manus came over to say they were going to sell their polly: they were short of grass for her, and it was a pity to sell her as she was, for she was in no condition for the market, as she wasn't coming for nearly five months. It would be as well for them to keep her on, and the best thing was to let her graze on the Doogans' land, and they could have the milk.

The two women arranged it like that. The Doogans and the Manuses had always been good neighbours. When the mother told Charlie, he said noting, but that night he kept away from Biddy Melly's, and tried another poaching effort by himself. He had very little success.

The salmon season was poor. After a month Charlie had only three pounds coming to him. On the way back from the Port he sold the donkey to Neil Rodgers for two pounds fifteen. That evening Mary Manus sold them the polly for five pounds ten.

That night Charlie went to Biddy Melly's, but Susan Manus was not there. She was at home making a dress for a neighbour girl.

CHAPTER 14

Charlie Doogan and Susan Manus escaped being together in the old way. It wasn't Phil Boyle's fault, for he made excuses and sought to leave them alone often. But, somehow, somebody always chanced along and the conversation that developed had more meaning to it than the few courtesy remarks that a courting couple might make to a neighbour, for people on an island don't press themselves on a pair of young folk. Charlie was to blame on occasion by drawing on topics about sailing boats and mainland happenings; other times it was Susan who gave life to the casual remarks by dragging in some pressing island topic. But neither of them gave any heed to the change and the island saw nothing of it.

On the night of the raffle for new windows for the school there was a good number of outside folk at the dance, and the island boys had to keep closer to their girls. This coming of outsiders often drove two people whose casual company-keeping had hitherto been aimless into a more definite understanding.

Charlie Doogan danced with Susan Manus a couple of times, and went over with her at midnight to have a sup of tea. It was a habit with the island girls close to the school to take a bunch of friends out with them like that, and to include the strangers. The old folk were always in bed when the midnight party came in, and even though the bed might happen to be in the kitchen, they never spoke.

Susan didn't wait to wash up after the tea, just bunched the bowls together and left them down in a basin. The other folk went out and set off back for the school. Naturally Charlie waited for Susie. That night Susan was wearing a new silk blouse, and a skirt that had been made for her by a new dressmaker in the Port. All the girls at the dance envied her for being so well-dressed. The girls did not see just as clearly as the boys that Susan Manus was a thundering fine girl, with her tall, supple figure, her fine glowing face, and deep, grey-blue eyes. Charlie Doogan was not the only man whose feelings had been quickened by a passing glimpse at Susan Manus at the raffle. And that very quickening had made Charlie unhappy.

Ever since the day his mother fainted, Charlie had been unsettled. He had emerged from the short reflection in the field a stern, purposeful man. His purpose was to drive back the starvation that was crushing his mother and his folk. If to achieve that purpose a means had been ready to his hand he would have won back his old buoyancy in a fortnight. But there was no task that his great strength could accomplish. He fished, slaving at the work, but there were few results, beyond occasional exhaustion. A strong man, with a purpose, without means to achieve it, he became restless. At first Charlie enjoyed occasional enthusiasm, but he soon learned to base his hopes less firmly on passing accidents. His restlessness was now settling down into a resolve. He would leave the island, and crash out something in the world outside. The task he had slaved at and the resolve he was forming both tended to prise him apart from Susan Manus. His fright in his mother's case had been the greatest emotion in his life so far. His love-making with Susan Manus had been more the deepening of a boy-and-girl palship than of the strong call of a mating instinct. It was only when the line of his thoughts for the future became clear to himself that he turned to consider Susan Manus. He was an islander, only at home among the boats on the island, and at peace when island life went smoothly. Life on the island included

Susan Manus. Looking forward, she continued to loom large in that life. Cherishing her when she was with him was not nearly so vital to him as the prospect of losing her was appalling. Suddenly there was a new hunger in him for her.

As he waited while she put away the delph, he struggled between the mood of the evening and the threat of to-morrow. They pulled the door to gently after them and turned down towards the sandbank to go back to the raffle. The turf-stack was on the way, and there was an old wooden lobster-tank beside it. They halted beside the box. They had often sat on it. The strains of the fiddle could be heard, and the tramp of the dancers. A girl's laughter floated across from the school yard. A piece of paper, caught in the wire netting of the hen-run, flapped softly in a light wind.

They faced each other beside the box. There was a smile on Susan's face. When she gazed at Charlie it ebbed. She was puzzled now, as she had been often of late; Charlie continued to be silent.

'What's over ye these times, Charlie?' she asked. 'Ye're strange these times,' she added.

'Strange?' he queried.

''Pon me word ye are. Ye look like a man with somethin' on his mind.'

'Maybe it's that,' he agreed. 'Maybe I have somethin' on me mind.' He was so still he made Susan nervous.

'Maybe more than you have things on their mind,' she said. He turned towards her sharply. 'What's in your mind, Susan?'

''Tis, I'm gettin' tired of the island,' she said, kicking a clod of turf. She had no thought of such a thing a moment before; indeed her words had been the first intimation, even to herself, that she had entertained such a thought.

'That's quare now, Susan,' he said, turning to face her squarely. 'Wasn't I thinkin' the same thing.'

Susan's eyes were full on his, and her face was flushed, and then without warning she turned and ran back home. It was some minutes before she opened the kitchen door, and then she watched Charlie for a good while through the bedroom window, and he standing at the turf-stack. When he had gone away, and she was in the middle of her night prayers, she began to sob. Charlie didn't go back to the dance, and it was late when he went in home.

CHAPTER 15

It was after a long series of failures that Charlie had luck again at Traighailla Strand. Phil Boyle and he made the effort that time, and their haul was mostly plaice. Charlie wasn't so dramatic with the money this time, and waited until morning before he gave it to his mother. There were seventeen shillings, but five shillings had to be kept for the priest, who was coming on stations, and a shilling for offerings to be paid over an old neighbour who was dying. However, there were still twelve shillings left.

Mary Doogan went down to the boat that evening to buy some provisions. Biddy Melly was there, when she produced her handful of silver to pay for her purchases.

'Are ye hearin' from the youngsters in the Lagan?' Biddy asked, her eyes on the money.

''Tis, then we didn't have a letter for a fortnight,' Mary answered innocently. 'And me mind is never at rest, an' won't pe till they're back with me,' she added gravely.

'Their few pounds'll come in handy at Hallow Eve,' Biddy said.

'Indeed an' it's it will,' Mary agreed. 'But still it's hard to send soft childer out to work among the stranger; but what else is for them?'

Biddy nodded. 'I see Mickey's wans are puttin' in a boarden floor in the room,' she said.

'Ye don't say,' Mary Doogan commented.

'Troth are they, an' talkin' of slatin' the room too. The wans in America is sendin' them a power of money.'

'It's good to see people gettin' on,' Mary said.

'The cow Jack Dooney bought is not in calf after all,' Biddy continued.

'Well, now, what d'ye think?'

'Jack's mad about it. He'd go back with her again for very little.'

'Men's no judge of a milch's cow,' Mary doogan decided. 'Jack wants some womankind about the house,' she added, with the merest suggestion of a smile.

'Well, the cow's on his hands anyway. For it's last night he was tellin' me,' Biddy said. lightly. 'Jack has a fine place, an' it's goin' to loss,' she continued. 'Jack's a discontented, fidgety nature of a man.'

'D'ye see him often, Biddy?' Mary Doogan said gently.

'Ye're as bad as the rest, Mary Doogan,' Biddy protested. 'Musha, not a better thing could happen the two of ye than fix it up,' Mary persisted.

Other women joined them then, and they exchanged snuff and gossip. When Mary left to go home she saw a strange boat standing in for the Point under Manus's. She paid little heed to it, for boats came in there often with school inspectors, and Congested Districts Board men, and the like. She went on home, eager to get ready the evening tea, which would be a treat for the children.

Neil Rodgers was spreading a newly-barked net when the strangers landed. He recognized them at once; Innisfree men whom he often met about the Port.

'It's new'ins to see ye on this island,' he greeted them, 'an' ye're welcome. Damn but Ned ye're standin' it well,' he commented, surveying the skipper.

'Ye're not doin' badly yerself, Neil, but between me an' you, I'd as soon not come to the island on the errand that brought me,' Ned said.

Neil made no comment.

'It's a wire that came in when I was in the Port. It's for the Doogans, an' I said I'd bring it,' Ned explained.

'About wan of the girls?' Neil asked.

'Aye, about the Nellie wan. She's dead.'

'Dead?' Neil questioned. 'God rest her soul,' he added. He put his hand to his hat, but he didn't take it off for fear the news would spread before the Doogans were told.

'Maybe you'd tell them,' Ned said, after a pause.

'I see Charlie over there. I'll tell Charlie,' Neil agreed.

'God help them,' Ned said, handing over the telegram.

'Amen! God knows,' Neil added.

The Innisfree boat did not delay, but went off home. Neil went across to Charlie. The latter saw him coming, and came down to meet him. Hughie, farther up the field, straightened on his spade, and stood looking down. Neither Charlie nor Neil spoke until they were face to face across the stone fence.

'There's bad news,' Neil said.

Charlie inclined his head.

'Nellie's dead,' Neil continued.

Charlie took off his cap. Neil handed him the wire. 'Nellie died this morning,' the wire read. Neil turned away and went home. Charlie saw Hughie hurrying down the field, and he leaned on the fence until he came up.

'It's Nellie,' Hughie said.

'It's Nellie,' Charlie agreed.

'Dead?'

'Dead?'

Hughie sat down on the edge of the drain. 'When'd she die?' he asked.

'This mornin'.' Charlie handed him the telegram. Then

they were both silent. They saw their mother appear in the doorway with a brush, driving back the hens. Then she shut the door.

Mary Manus was standing at the door of Neil's house, talking to Mary Neil Charlie went over home. The mother was scraping a pot when he went in. She spoke without looking up. 'Shut the door after ye to keep out them hens. They're in over the place if ye give them a chink. Ye'd think not a bite they got this fortnight.'

Charlie shut the door. 'I got a whole shopful of things,' the mother continued, 'an' I got a stick of liquorice for Nabla. It always eases her breathin'.'

Without speaking Charlie went up and sat on the side of the bed. The sight of his mother, happy in the excitement of her purchases, unnerved him. She looked up sharply.

'Ye're sick, Charlie,' she said, getting to her feet, and hurrying over to him. She laid a hand on his forehead.

He wanted to tell her gently, but he couldn't. Her face was very close to his when he spoke. 'It's Nellie,' he said. Her eyes searched his. 'Nellie's dead, died this mornin'.'

For a moment she stood still; then she staggered back from him. As she sank to the ground he caught her.

'Is Nellie dead? Is me child dead?' she whispered.

'She's dead,' he sobbed, his restraint gone.

Just then the neighbour women came in, and he left his mother to them and went out to the byre.

CHAPTER 16

Work on the island stopped with the spreading of the news about Nellie Doogan. The men went straight from the fields to Doogan's. The women hurriedly washed their faces and put on their shawls the same as if they were going to Mass. When good news comes, people crowd in in any way, but when a death is announced the women always take off their aprons, and put their shawls on their heads before they go to the wakehouse. Charlie was still in the byre when Hughie came in to him. Hughie was dry-eyed.

'There'll be things wanted for the wake,' Hughie said.

Charlie nodded.

'An' won't we bring Nellie home?' Hughie asked.

'We will,' Charlie said.

'Won't there be money wanted for that?' Hughie probed.

'There will. We'll have to sell the cow.' He discussed it with Neil Rodgers and then Hughie drove the cow down to the boat, where Charlie and Neil were waiting to take her out. Neil bent the left front foot, and got it in over the gunwale, resting it on the dry seaweed that had been put there on purpose. Then Hughie gave the cow a tap with a rod and she walked into the boat, and stood quietly, swishing her tail, as the boat put off.

Phil Boyle and Neil Rodgers's son got busy about the wakehouse. They cleared the nets from the end of the kitchen, and carried in and arranged big stones to rest planks on for seats. Young Rodgers went over to Biddy Melly's for a form, to put along under the window, while Phil Boyle took one over from Manus's, and placed it alongside the kitchen bed. The women were busy arranging other things. Susan Manus sent Phil Boyle over to their barn to mix a bucket of lime until she would whitewash the gable over the fire, where brown spots were showing through. Later she helped her mother to arrange a white coverlet on the kitchen bed, and to pin white linen round it. Instead of black crosses they took down the crosses of blessed straw from the rafters, dusted them, and pinned them to the bedposts.

Mary Manus and Hannah Neil Rodgers consulted, as to whether candles should be lighted, since the corpse wasn't in the house. In the end they decided against it. Mary Doogan, herself, sat in the corner, crying softly to herself, listening to the words of the neighbours as they dropped in one after the other. Susan Manus made tea for them all, and she without knowing the joy Mary Doogan thought to take out of baking that flour and wetting that tea.

It was near dark when Charlie and Neil Rodgers came back. As the fair was next day in Dungloe, they had little trouble in getting rid of the cow. Hughie O'Donnell had helped them, and besides that he wired to a friend of his in the Lagan to help Sally get the corpse to the train. They had pipes and tobacco and loaves of bread with them. When the pipes and tobacco were placed on the kitchen table, Mary Doogan burst into a passionate fit of weeping. The neighbour women were glad she cried.

'Let her empty her heart,' Mary Manus said, with a knowledge of the day she had cried her drowned son, in her mind to give her wisdom.

At midnight they said the fifteen decades, just the same as if it was an ordinary wake, and many young folk sat up with the Doogans until morning, but there were no games played, like is done when an old person is dead. In the morning a string of boats took the islanders out to meet the corpse. Mary Doogan just happened to be standing in front of the carriage where Sally was, and she fainted when she embraced her. There was a little delay before taking the coffin out of the van. They weren't sure whether it should be four Doogans would take up the coffin, the same as if it was being carried out of a wakehouse on the island, and there were only three Doogan men on the platform. A commercial traveller came forward and said his name was Doogan, and he helped them for the first few yards. After that any four men would do to carry the corpse.

They carried Nellie Doogan's coffin down the slip, and put it into the boat that had taken her to Dungloe, when she went to the hiring fair. Sally sat beside the coffin, and the women leaned forward eagerly, to listen to her story of how Nellie had died from neglected appendicitis, and how she had lain all by herself, for days, in a barn loft.

Next day Nellie Doogan was buried beside her father in the churchyard in Arranmore.

CHAPTER 17

The evening after the funeral the Doogans were by themselves around the fire, before it was right dark. The children fell asleep and were carried off to bed. Sally, Hughie, Charlie and the mother were left together.

'What about me goin' back to finish me time?' Sally said. 'That'd be better than doin' with the thirty shillin's he's givin' me for all I done.'

'I don't want a child belongin' to me to go back to the Lagan. When I think of me wee girl, an' not wan to reach her a drink-'

'My place is different,' Sally interrupted. 'Nellie's master was awful rough. I didn't like him the first sight I saw of him, only he was near to my place. He came to me early in the mornin'. "Ye're too thin in the shanks," says he, lookin' down at me legs, an' half liftin' me skirt. An' he put his hands on me shoulders, like he was feelin' how much flesh was on me bones.'

'True as God, I'll get me fingers on that man yet,' Charlie said.

'I'd do it if I was to tramp the whole way, if I was a man,' Sally said.

'Whist, Sally,' the mother remonstrated. 'It's goin' to be a hard time for us now, if God hasn't said otherwise,' she continued, looking into the fire. 'Ye're without milk again. It's a plentiful time with the neighbours,' she added, 'so the milk won't be the worst.'

'I'll go to Scotland now, anyway,' Charlie said. 'But it's what ye're to do for the next couple of weeks puzzles me.'

'Who'll take out the crops?' the mother asked.

'Hughie and Sally can do that. 'I'll spend a day or two cuttin' scraws to cover the praties. After that it's easy. Then I'll go. There's nothin' else to be done,' he added. He got up and went outside. Sally followed him out.

'Under God, Charlie, there's not a bite under the roof.'

'Nothin' at all left?' he asked hopelessly.

'Nothin',' she said. 'There's tea an' sugar over from the wake, but that's all.'

'That's all, is it?' he asked her.

She looked at him sharply. 'What's wrong with ye, Charlie?' she asked.

He was looking up at the sky. 'What does it all mean, Sally? Did ye see the way mother looked sittin' there in the corner? An' then there's the morrow, an' the next day, an' every day, till I get somethin' earned.'

'Maybe there'd be eggs,' Sally said.

'The disorder carried off all the hens.'

'An' is there no knittin'?'

'Me mother couldn't get any this month.'

They were both silent. 'Go in home, Sally. I'll have flour for the mornin',' he said suddenly.

'How'll ye get it, Charlie?'

'Never ye mind how, I'll get flour.'

He walked away from her, and went cautiously over to the Point. He carried a curragh down to the edge of the strand, and set off in it. He burst into the Goods Shed at Burton-port, and took a pack of flour. He came in with it under his arm.

'What's that, Charlie?' the mother shot at him. 'What's that?'

'A bag of flour,' he said carelessly. 'A bag of flour – an' it was rightly come by,' he added, but he didn't leave it in the kitchen as usual, but he took it up with him to the room, and set it on a block against the gable. Then he went to bed.

And now Charlie was to go to Scotland on the morrow. He was taking his fare out of the thirty shillings that had been sent to Sally from the Lagan. He was cutting scraws to leave handy for covering the pits, for cutting scraws would be too heavy for Hughie. He had begun to speculate on whether he might not have sufficient cut. He leaned on his spade and gazed around him.

It was a lusty evening. In the west the bronze-bordered sun glowed above the ocean. The sea throbbing to a flood-tide slammed wavelets against the rocks. The waters of the Bay darkened here to shade, there brightened to a sunbeam. A few fields away Neil Rodgers straightened his back to rest from his job of fixing torn gaps in a ring net.

Suddenly Charlie's relaxed figure went tense. Something in the water of the bay caught and gripped his attention; just a dark spot in the sea, where no cloud could be reflected, and a lone seagull circling over it. Away up, high above the seagull, a gannet, careering home, halted suddenly, and spun round as though from an impact. The circling gannet acted on Charlie's stiffened body like a shock. His legs uncrossed; one heavy booted foot descended on the spade like a piston and sank it to the ears in the ground. Then the gannet struck, nose-diving from the clouds, right into the centre of the black patch.

Charlie was running now, making straight for Neil. Neil saw him before he had covered half the distance separating them and dropped his work. He waited for Charlie to come up.

'Herrin', herrin',' Charlie said excitedly.

Neil had not seen anything, but he knew Charlie. "M'ere Cormac,' he shouted, in a voice as charged with feeling as Charlie's.

A bare-legged youngster came running out of the house.

'Run ye boy, an' tell Phil Boyle, an' Manus, an' Donal to hurry. Herrin',' he added. 'An' say nothin' till ye tell them first.'

It was Neil's crew running to the beach that set the island going. The shout of 'Herrin', herrin',' went from field to field, from house to house. Neil had reached the dark spot that marked the herring shoal, and had shot his nets in a ring round it before any other boat came up. There was a tussle for second place. Jack the Post, from Arran, won it. His train made a circle outside Neil's. Soon a half score of trains were set round about.

'Is it herrin', d'ye think?' a fisherman shouted to Neil.

Charlie Doogan's nostrils quivered for a moment as he sniff-ed again. 'Ye could cut the smell of them here,' he said, and then Jack the Post shouted, pointing to Neil's nets.

Two of Neil's nets had sunk. The herring shoal was in motion.

Neil set to work to haul rapidly. Three nets cargoed their boat. Young Hughie Doogan, Sally and Neil's wife were coming up with a second boat. The other two nets were taken on to her.

Then one of Jack's nets sank, and so the work went on and the excitement grew.

For the herring had come in at last, and the cry rang through the two parishes.

'They're ringin' herrin' ! They're ringin' herrin'! Up and out; up and out!'

CHAPTER 19

A week's frenzied reaping of a great harvest. The coast hummed with activity. Men worked night and day. The market opened greedy jaws, and prices held. Families leaped from naked poverty to comparative wealth. Among such were the Doogans. The lucky opening had been followed by a series of lucky chance shots. Tea, sugar, flour, tobacco were all available now. For the first time in his life Charlie Doogan sat at the table, and cut bread for himself. Hitherto each cake of bread had been divided out by the mother, now, he, Hughie and Sally were free to cut for themselves. Charlie remembered when it had been his ambition to sit just there and cut bread, and butter it himself, and eat until he was satisfied.

And the mother; the night Charlie came home and flung a bundle of notes into her lap, as she sat on her creepy in the corner, she gasped. Never in her life had she seen so much money. She counted with something akin to dismay. Twenty-three pounds for a week's fishing, and all the catches not paid for.

The night a council was held. A new cow would be bought at once.

The next fair day was only three days away. Manus O'Donnell went out with Mary Doogan to help her buy. Mary herself would decide on the shape of the cow, and whether all her teats were right, whether her skin was dry, and whether she was easy to milk. Manus was a good judge of a cow's mouth.

They bought a cow from a Loughanure man. Mary liked her well enough, but one of her teats was a bit small. She was a young cow, and the man that sold her explained that his wife died just the day before the cow calved, her first calf, and that it was the children milked her, and that they didn't milk her well. Mary believed him. It was a fault she could overcome in time. To be sure the cow was a bit thin, but her skin was good. All she wanted was her meat, and they had that to give her indeed. Her keep was going to loss – a farm without a four-footed beast on it. They paid the money and took the cow home.

Mary Manus was down to them as soon as they landed.

She blessed the new cow. She asked the price; they made her guess. She was ten shillings too high. That pleased Mary Doogan. Biddy Melly met them next. She guessed fifteen shillings too little. Manus flared up. He had taken a couple of 'treats' in Hughie O'Donnell's after paying for the cow. 'Good,' he said. 'It's yerself'd say it. Ye were askin' more than that for the dyin' bag of rattlin' bones ye had out last fair day.'

'Arrah, have sense,' Mary admonished. 'Indeed, Biddy, many's the time the like of her could be got the price ye say, but everythin' was dear the day,' which was true. The Doogans were not the only family to whom the herring would bring the sup of milk.

Towards the end of the second week the heavy catches were fewer. Neil's crew were still in luck. They caught another cargo on Friday night. Saturday was a day of great commotion in the fishing village. Little rolls of notes were handled here and there, men getting paid at the buyers' offices, and then coming out to count over their rolls to their eager women folk. It was a light-hearted, boisterous, not too sober crowd. Here and there a quarrelsome person made a great noise. An occasional blow was struck, but night found the island boats making for home, and a glowering heavens, low and threatening, hanging over a sea beginning to gurn and toss.

CHAPTER 20

It was night time in Inniscara. The boats were clustered on the beach, far beyond the sweep of the waves that dashed up the strand, pushing a fringe of froth in front, and dragging back into the boiling cauldron outside reluctant pebbles that grumbled as they went. Away to the west, driving clouds raced across the face of the moon, and stray stars peeped through changing gaps in the tremulous sky. From the back of the island came the roar of heavy breakers smashing against the grey rocks, breaking with a boom, or hammering the sandy embankment with a thud; over the fields, darkness, with here and there banks of thickened shadows sheltering along mud fences from the moon.

This climax had arrived after a whole fortnight of squalls and rain, and waiting. Hope of renewing fishing was now gone, and so on a Sunday night the island folk grouped and gossipped around the firesides. Manus O'Donnell's was full of old men; in Biddy Melly's the young folk were gathered. Charlie Doogan was in Biddy Melly's, and so was Susan Manus. Phil Boyle was there too, and was busy teasing Biddy about Jack Doney. Jack had been merry in Burtonport on the last pay night, and had come down the street with his arm around Biddy, an incident that would keep Jack at his own fireside for some time. He daren't face the chaff in Biddy's, and the old men in Manus's would be even more merciless.

'Oh, be me sowl, Biddy!' Phil Boyle burst out in reply to an attempt by Biddy to thrust the matter aside, 'Jack wasn't drunk. I was with him the whole evenin'. We had only four drinks, an' it was only halfs Jack was drinkin'. Four halfs never made him drunk. He had only enough to give him nerve. A quare ould grin he had on him, an' be me sowl, Biddy, nobody noticed any huff on yerself. It's a go.'

'Can a body not help a drunk man to a boat, but the whole island is puttin' meanin' into it? Susan Manus linked yerself to a boat last Christmas Eve, and nobody tried pushin' ye into each other's arms next day.'

Phil blushed and looked at Susan. Susan laughed, and then stole a glance at Charlie.

'An' Biddy was quiltin' last week,' Susan Manus said, thrusting back the chaff. 'It's brave an' quiet herself an' Jack done it. Only for the wee drop of drink it'd never come out.'

'Ye'll trouble the life out of the poor man,' Biddy said, going out with a drink to a calf.

'God only knows where the herinn's'll be after the night,' Phil Boyle said, taking a coal in the tongs to light his pipe. 'Maybe it's in further they'd be driven, ye never know,' Hugh Rodgers said. 'Maybe it's into Traighenna they'd be after this.'

'It's off somewhere else they'll be,' Charlie Doogan decided. 'Maybe we have our ration of them, an' they're wanted badly somewhere else.'

Charlie's remark, deep in its significance to himself, was laughed aside. Only Susan Manus, alive to a new elusiveness in Charlie, puckered her brow to give heed to it.

'An' who would do the dividin' round the coast?' she asked, looking into the fire. 'God, would it be?' Nobody answered for a moment.

'If it is, a couple of Saturday pay nights is what made Him shift out of here then,' Phil Boyle said, in returning to his banter, Biddy Melly having come back in the meantime.

'When ye find women hookin' men they never were given any licence to mix with, down the public street...'

'Arrah, damn on ye! it's not the nerve to hoult a girl ye'd have herself, ye poor slat mara,' Biddy said, and hurled the mossy end of a turf at him.

A great blast of wind blew ashes out into their faces.

'Ye're talkin',' Charlie Doogan said, getting up on his elbow, 'But it's blowin' a livin' gale. I'll dander over an' see how the boats are tied down.' He glanced at Susan Manus as he got to his feet.

'Go out an' don't keep him standin' in the could for ye at the gable,' Biddy Melly said to Susan.

'Go out yerself,' Susan said, blushing.

Phil Boyle changed the subject, but now and again he sat looking at Susan, his expression thoughtful, and a bit sad. Phil was puzzled.

CHAPTER 21

That night the Doogans were rapped up by Peggy's husband, Miley Ferry. He came to the room window and Charlie heard him. He hopped to the kitchen in the bare feet and opened the sheltered door. The mother heard the bolt being drawn.

'Are ye asleep, Mary?' Miley said.

'Am not,' Mary said.

'Peggy asked me come over for ye.'

There was the creak of bedboards and then the pat of feet on the floor. 'I'll be with ye now. Did she say I was to hurry?'

'She didn't like to risk waitin' 'til mornin'.'

'Did ye call yer mother?'

'I'm goin' on there next. I'll leave ye over first.'

'Well, I'm ready now.'

The two went out. Charlie went back to bed. It was late when he got up. He lay and lazed. He heard Sally make peace between Nabla and Sheila. He heard the rattle of the bowls in the dish as she washed up.

Sheila put her head up the room door, and glanced at Charlie. Seeing him awake she smiled. Charlie signalled to her with his finger, and she ran to him, creeping into bed beside him. 'Is the breakfast ready?'

She nodded, with all the seriousness of three years. 'An' Sally has pancakes for ye on a plate at the fire,' she added. 'Did you get pancakes?'

She nodded.

Charlie whispered to her, playing at secrecy. 'Run down an' whisper to Sally to give me me breakfast in bed, an' me an' you'll have more pancakes.'

The child disengaged herself from Charlie's arm. Then she stopped suddenly. 'Ye sick, Charlie?' she asked.

Charlie drew her hesd close to his and whispered again. 'Lazy.'

She drew back and looked at him with wide eyes. He nodded. She clapped her hands, and laughed, and ran to the kitchen. He chuckled when he heard Sally — 'What are ye sayin'? What?' And then Sally appeared at the room door, her head bent to the whispering Sheila. Charlie nodded to her. She straightened up and laughed.

'Not a bit more sense ye have than the child,' she said, going to the kitchen.

When she brought up the tea, Sheila shut the room door, and then scampered back to bed beside Charlie. She, took every other sup out of Charlie's bowl. Then he sent the child down with the bowl and plate, and he dressed rapidly.

His mother had not come home. Peggy was still ill. She was expecting a baby. Charlie went out. He cast his eye over the beach to where the boats were clustered. Then he saw a crowd of men at Manus's gable close by. After a moment's hesitation he left the shelter of his own side wall, and made his away across to Manus's.

A shower of hail sent them all into the house. Mary Manus was sitting in the corner knitting. Susan was baking. Her eyes and Charlie's met; she nodded to him.

Manus was the old man of the island. He always sat in the corner near the bed. It was said of him he never sat anywhere else in his own house. His eye sought out Charlie. 'Here's himself,' he greeted. 'A hell of a stormy day it was he come. I was on the bow oar. I was skinned and had to eat standin' for months after.'

Charlie shared a chair with Neil Rodgers.

'It was a day an' a half,' Manus continued, 'but doctors was never wanted much them days. We were late for the boyo too. It's only since these mainland women began bein' brought to the island that the doctors was wanted.'

'It's a pity some of ye men didn't have a trial of twins,' Mary Manus said; 'ye would know more what ye be sayin'.'

Miley Ferry came to the door, Mary Neil Rodgers hanging on his arm.

'If ye can 't get a doctor for Peggy,' Mary said quietly, 'she'll be in a bad way if it's not God's will.'

CHAPTER 22

There was a sudden noise of the shuffling of nailed boots on the cement floor, as the men got to their feet. Manus reached for his stick, and stood up too. Except for Charlie Doogan, he was yet the tallest man in the house.

'Neil's boat's the handiest that'll stand heavy sea,' he said sharply, 'them iron bars of ours is yer best ballast, Charlie Doogan on the helm, Phil Boyle, Hughie Rodgers, Dominick, John Dubh, and Neil, that's yer crew.'

'It's gettin' off'll be the job,' Neil Rodgers said, leaving the gable.

All the men on the island streamed down to the beach. The boat was got ready. They shoved her down to the edge of the foam, and halted. Wave after wave, rising up into crests that reached mountains high, exhausted itself at their feet. A heavy breaker, frothing to look like an avalanche, rushed toward them. As it receded they raced with the boat after it. Terrific gusts of wind flicked the foam in their faces, blinding them, or showing the smooth, tinkling, rounded stones momentarily. The receding water met the incoming wave, and under the conflict of forces the swell reared its head higher and higher, and then burst into a frothing crest, pitching forward with a sound, like a throatal growl from the live earth. The line of men by the boat kept her bow to it, but the wave boiled in across the gunwale, washed over the men who hung to the sides, and carried all backwards. The ready Neil Rodgers threw the stern cable to a group higher up the beach, and they, racing back, held on when the swell swept out, thus helped to stem the swell on the swamped boat. Drenched, spluttering, soaking, the men gazed at one another. To launch now was impossible. The boat would go the bottom like a stone. Another wave was gathering, now it was pitching upward, curling at the top, now it was boiling, now it was hissing, growling, tearing down on the beach.

'Get back,' Charlie Doogan ordered. And they raced back, leaving the boat to the mountain of foam that buried her, while they hauled on the cable to take her forward with the wave.

Manus shook his head. 'I never did see just the like of it,' he said.

They made another attempt over under Mickey Mor's, where a rock split the waves, but again, beaten, drenched men retreated before mountains of bad-tempered seas, leaving behind them this time a sunken boat.

'Blast it!' Charlie Doogan said, shaking his fist at the waves, 'it's like suds; there's no body to it.'

They trailed back to Manus's; some went home to change, to others a change of clothing was brought by the women-folk, who knew that the men would wait to snatch any chance that might arise. But the day passed and the conditions worsened. The storm smote blows, like world impacts, with lulls between that were like gasps for breath, while the sea rose and swept the island, filling the air with salt, and sound, and foam, and fear. And then the gaunt channel rocks merged in a haze where trembling clouds reached down to thickening spray, knitting into a shade that deepened and darkened, until night fell down on the madness and the dread, the helplessness and the suffering. And there were the men of the island gathered in Manus's, and the little street of island houses, and Miley Ferry's with the two lights, one in the kitchen and one in the room, a thing that never happens but when there is sickness in a house.

Morning, and woman still gathered in Miley Ferry's; the stolid group of silent men still clustered among the boats; and the breakers towering higher and higher.

CHAPTER 23

Charlie Doogan's concern for Peggy was deep and strong. Indeed, all his fondest ties had centred in her until she had left to marry Miley Ferry. After that he was almost a stranger at his own hearth. It is true his relationship with her of late years had not been as in the days before she married Miley. She was his champion in those far-off days, when he was struggling for the freedom of his middle teens. It was she used to watch for him while he shaved; she bought him his first white collar – it was for a Patrick's Night dance in Arranmore. She often wheedled an odd sixpence for him on a day of a regatta. And she alone took pride in his great strength – he remembered how she encouraged him in his weight-throwing and rowing. He was remembering Peggy across the casual years that had passed since he had drifted. And now, she wanted a doctor, how badly he didn't know. Sickness was beyond the range of his experience, and its place in his understanding was vague. He was troubled about Peggy, not really roused on her behalf. He had laboured to launch the boat, as he would have laboured in any attempt, on such a day, putting the whole weight of his body into the struggle, troubled, but not roused.

He wished to see his mother. He set off across the beach to Peggy's. She was in the kitchen when he went in. Tears were trickling down her face when she looked at him, and just then Peggy was crying, her great, unrestrained crying, that was so like a child's. Charlie had heard grown-up people cry on occasions at wakes, or a convoy, but it had been the crying of grown-up people. This was different. Not since the day Peggy cut her foot on a black bottle had he heard sobbing that came straight from the heart like that. He laid hard fingers on his mother's arm. 'Is that our Peggy?' he asked, almost hissed. The mother buried her face in her hands, and her body shook.

'It's her, and she won't be long in it, either,' Mary Neil Rodgers said.

'I never knew, God, I never knew,' Charlie said, running out of the house.

CHAPTER 24

The men saw Charlie come out of Miley's, and come towards them. He seemed scarcely to bend to the blast, but to sweep through it without staggering. A sense of a new force let loose among the storm came to them.

'Heavens above, but that boy minds me of his grandfather!' Manus O'Donnell said, and then they were all silent until he came to them. He sought out Manus O'Donnell.

'Manus,' he said, 'you were a great man in a curragh; how'd ye get off the island?'

Manus was silent for a moment. ''Twas a day like this yer grandfather, God rest his soul, went from the Point,' Manus said.

'Ye were there, Manus?' Charlie said.

'I was,' Manus agreed quietly.

'Ye planted the curragh on a swell that was sweepin' in an' he was off with the back-wash. I heard him tell it. I mind fine.' He looked at the beach. 'It's a question of bein' through the first breaker 'fore it bursts.'

'It's that,' Manus said; 'an' of not lettin' the next or the next catch ye with its broken top.'

'I'm goin' in a curragh,' Charlie said.

The men moved on their feet; nobody spoke.

'Ye'll help me get the curragh planted. Take it out in yer arms to where the wave spendin' itself will about reach yer waists. Ye can have ropes on ye to keep ye from the wash pullin' ye out. I'll scoot out an' try an' get across the neck of the first wave before it bursts deep. Then I'll let it drive me. I must do that.'

Nobody stirred. Charlie turned to Phil.

'Help me, Phil.'

'It's madness, Charlie,' Phil said, taking a chew of tobacco.

Charlie turned from them and made towards a curragh.

'I was waitin' for this; he's his grandfather over again; God bless him, an' his stock were men,' Manus said.

They watched him untie the ropes. Phil sighed. 'Ah, well, in God's Name,' he said, crossing himself.

The others followed Phil's lead. They carried the curragh to the Point. Charlie kicked off his boots.

'Take off the gansey,' Manus advised.

Four men with ropes round their waists held the curragh. The group on the shore held the other ends of the ropes. A wave boiled over and swept forward.

'Now,' Charlie said.

The four men raced into the surf. The curragh floated in their hands; Charlie flopped into it. He shot out with the first ebb of the wave. The staggering men were helped ashore, going reluctantly backward, their eyes on the curragh.

CHAPTER 25

He got across the first wave just as foam began to rise from its crest. He was going down its neck when it broke. Into the trough in front of him a wave was tumbling white. He

64

floundered for a moment in the trough, rose hurriedly to the next swell, and again just managed to get across, not, however, until he had shipped some water. It was a mighty tussle, full of skill, and strength, and blessed with luck. Once clear of the surf, he drove before the storm, delaying, hurrying, once or twice trusting blindly, but racing, racing across the waters. His black, hatless head, his set, granite-hued face dripping wet; strong, supple arms, fingers of steel. And as he drove, the storm seemed suddenly to sing of triumph, to back him up against the waters, and the latter to roll after him and shoot up challengingly before him, not because they could win, but because they had the persistence of the stupid. He shouted; he knew not why, but he shouted... just opened his mouth and roared, plying his paddle with grand stroke, and god-like confidence. He growled when a swell slipped water into the curragh; laughed when he broke the face of a crumbling wave. And then he thought of Peggy. 'And she won't be long in it either.' Mary Neil's words were in the blast. He drove his bending paddle deeper into the tossing water, and forged forward, using strength mostly, almost scorning to use caution.

He landed under the shelter of the Point near Burtonport bare-footed, soaked in salt water, and now the thought of Peggy so strong on him, that for the first time since he left the island he was frightened.

'Was I long? Was I long?' he muttered. And then he raced up the fields to the doctor's house.

CHAPTER 26

Doctor Wilson was in his third year as dispensary doctor in the Rosses. His sister, Ruth, spent a great deal of her time with him. She had long wished to live in the Rosses and to know its people. It was a desire born of the Abbey

Theatre, and fostered by short trips to Kerry and Conne-mara. She had made friends with the local people, especially with the fishermen, who let her accompany them when they went out, testifying to her popularity by declaring that she brought them luck. The women folk, however, held her a little apart; their thoughts and their lives were largely matters for speculation; she had little access to their minds, and she knew it. An elderly aunt lived with the brother and sister. She interested herself in their creature comforts, and considered she was exercising guardianship over them while they grew up and got sense.

During the long storm the doctor had been out but little, except to go daily to the post-office; Ruth went with him in the car to visit a few patients. They were now collected round a bright fire, and immersed in the post. Ruth was absorbed in the story of a swimming match in Dublin; the doctor was idly perusing an advertising leaflet.

'I see the Prince of Wales had a wonderful reception in Canada,' the aunt said, speaking out of the folds of the *Daily Mail*. 'Dear me, how he works! I think he is just splendid.'

'I can't get over Stasia Byrne winning that half-mile. I could always swim rings round her,' Ruth said.

Puff, puff, from the doctor's pipe.

'How the natives love the prince. One old fellow walked two hundred miles to be present at the reception. That's a lesson to some of those at home,' thus the aunt.

'Stasia will be up in her hat. But what a freak photo of her! Give me a cigarette, Dick.'

'Ruth, dear, you're smoking too many cigarettes,' the aunt objected, without laying down her paper.

The brother and sister smiled, and the latter stretched out her crossed legs to rest them on a chair, and reached for a book. 'Let me get back to my *Conqueror*,' she said. 'What a lovable type that man Hamilton was. 'Pon my word, one would be justified in anything to beget a son like that.'

'Ruth!'

'Auntie!'

'You hurt me,' the aunt complained.

Ruth sat up and threw impulsive arms around her aunt, gave her a hug, and then lay back again. 'I'll be good, Auntie. It's that storm; don't you feel it? It has the sea raging, the earth trembling, it can't leave me serene. Moses-"

The exclamation wrung from her by the sudden hammering at the door. And then the room door was flung open. 'My God! The Danes have landed – a Viking,' she added with vigour, commenting on the man who had entered. He was tall; he was drenched; he was excited; his face was pale, rugged, granite-like. His hair was black and short, scattered irregularly, as heavy rain flattens hair. He was bare-footed; he wore a sleeveless vest. It was Charlie Doogan.

The doctor and the aunt got to their feet. Charlie spoke first.

'My sister's very bad,' he said. 'Ye're wanted, quick.'

'Where to?'

'Inniscara.'

'Good heavens!' the doctor commented.

'She's very bad,' Charlie urged.

'Confinement?' the doctor asked.

Charlie nodded.

Then the aunt spoke. 'The doctor couldn't go now. He'll go the very first minute it settles,' she assured him.

Charlie's eyes were on the speaker, then they shifted to Ruth. He said: 'They say she'll die if the doctor doesn't come now.'

The doctor walked to the window. 'How did you come?' he asked.

'A curragh,' Charlie said.

'What?' Ruth protested. 'A curragh? You never came in a curragh in that?'

'We broke two boats,' Charlie said simply. 'It was the only chance.'

Tears started suddenly in Ruth's eyes, just a sudden passing wave of emotion.

'How am I to get there?' the doctor asked thoughtfully.

'There's drifters down here; wan of them'll go,' Charlie said.

Ruth nodded. 'I was thinking of that,' she said. 'The *Gola Star* boys will go first shot.'

'But the doctor couldn't go out in that,' the aunt persisted. The doctor put his hand on her shoulder. 'That lunatic came in a curragh.'

'She's very bad, doctor,' Charlie pleaded; 'if we could hurry.'

'I'll be ready in a minute,' the doctor decided.

'I'm coming,' Ruth said.

The doctor halted, with his hand on the knob of the door, and frowned.

'Fiddlesticks, Dick. Now, be a sport.'

'Well, well, if the drifter goes –' the doctor yielded.

'It will,' she said. *Gola Star* will go.'

The doctor hurried off to get ready.

'This poor man will get his death,' the aunt said.

Ruth looked at Charlie. No half-drowned man ever was so imposing, she thought. 'You'll have to get a change of things,' she said.

But he only smiled at her, and shook his head. 'I'll have the drifter ready, an' we'll be waitin',' and before they could say anything more to him he was gone.

CHAPTER 27

The crew of the *Gola Star* didn't hesitate for a moment; islanders themselves, they were only too glad to help another fisherman. It happened that they had steam up, for they were about to push out to the shelter of Rutland. As soon as the doctor and his sister arrived, they put off. Charlie's curragh was already on board. The Captain pointed it out to Ruth.

'Just how did that live through them waves?' he asked, nodding out to the bay, where white-capped mountains sported. 'He came in that.'

'He came in that,' the Captain assured her. 'The like of it happens just once in fifty years, an' it's only them sees it believes it. Nobody need have told me if I hadn't seen it with me own eyes.'

'And it was just his sister who was ill?' she said.

'His sister,' the Captain said.

Charlie was in the bow, he was dressed now, his body leaning forward eagerly, impatience pressing him. Ruth came and stood by his side. It was a few minutes before he became aware of her presence. He smiled, but he did not speak.

'Did you count on this?' she asked.

'I thought of it; I hoped some motor-boat would be about. It's landin' the doctor'll be the job,' and then as if struck by an idea he left her abruptly to discuss plans with the skipper. She stood there, the spray hurling against her oilskins, continuously her mind filled with the picture of the curragh and its lone pilot riding these crests.

Charlie came back to her. She put her lips close to his ear. 'Did you fix it?'

He nodded.

They both became silent. It was difficult to exchange remarks. Soon the island came into view, with its row of houses, then the beach, and then, hustle and running figures. He saw somebody running to Miley's. He took courage from the movements. They were not activities round about a corpse. Peggy was still alive.

The steamer stood down close to the strand. The shelter of her broke the force of the waves on the beach. A curragh was swamped in an attempt to launch. A second effort succeeded. The doctor flopped in, timing his jump nicely. They rushed him ashore.

Phil Boyle came alongside in a second curragh. Charlie and Ruth were standing side by side. Charlie jumped and landed safely. As he staggered up the beach, there was a shout from the boat. Ruth standing on the deck, her skirts flattened against her legs, raised an arm and waved.

'Take me ashore,' she called.

Charlie scratched his head.

'Charlie Doogan,' she called, 'take me ashore.'

'Seo, well,' Charlie said to Phil.

They got off safely. They came alongside. A swell was sweeping round the stern. The curragh swung to it. Charlie delayed signalling to Ruth, waiting for the wave to pass, but she, considering the position favourable, jumped. The curragh swung from under her; she landed flop in the sea. Diving out of the boat like a duck, Charlie went in after her. He bumped against her down there. They came to the surface on the back of a crest. Their eyes met.

'Good swimmer,' she said.

They kept together. They struggled shorewards. They appeared on the back of a wave. A human chain had been formed; they were grabbed. Before they were quite clear of the surf they halted. Ruth's hand was in Charlie's.

'I wanted a dip, and I got it,' she said.

'By the Lord, she's stuff,' Manus O'Donnell commented.

CHAPTER 28

Ruth Wilson was taken over to Manus O'Donnell's, where Susan provided her with a change of clothing. The two girls sat on Susan's bed, while Ruth drank a glass of hot milk.

Charlie Doogan went home. Sally pale as a ghost, partly from cold, for she had been on the beach for hours, partly from fright, for she thought Charlie was drowned, was hanging on to his side. Charlie's uncle was in the house. 'That was a daft trick, takin' that girl off,' the uncle said. 'Maybe so,' Charlie said tiredly, going towards the room door. He staggered against the table, recovered himself, and then sank to the floor, almost completely unconscious.

'Oh, Mother of God, Jesus, Mary and Joseph! Charlie's dead,' Sally screamed.

The uncle, who had been going out for turf, ran to raise him. 'Sally,' he said, 'run a chailleach over to Manus's. He has a sup of whiskey – run.' He pulled Charlie across in front of the fire, and began to rub his arms, calling to him the while.

Sally fought her way through the storm to Manus's. She burst into the house just as Ruth and Susan came up from the room. She was sobbing, and in panic.

'Charlie's dead,' she said; 'he fell on the floor, dead.'

'Dead?' Manus shouted. 'Damn the dead, more'n me. Played out.' He dived under his pillow, and took out a small black bottle. 'There's a glass in that. Run now. Here, girl.' He handed the bottle to Ruth, who was between him and Susan. 'Run ye, an' spill this into him. *Run.*'

The three girls, arms linked, ran out and raced before the storm to Doogan's. The uncle had got him undressed, and into the kitchen bed. Ruth placed the bottle on his lips, and got him to swallow the whiskey. She put pot lids to heat in the fire, put them in flannel and placed them around him. Charlie opened his eyes; he recognized Ruth. 'You beat me,' he said, with a wan smile.

'Don't, Charlie,' she protested; 'I feel mean. I'd forgotten about that fight going out.'

He turned his head away. Soon he was asleep. Before going back to Manus's, Ruth tiptoed over to the bed. Susan and Sally were in the room for the moment. Only the children were round the fire. 'My big, wild man of the sea,' she said. 'My big, wild man of the sea.' And hearing the others coming down from the room, she stepped back almost guiltily from the bed.

A short time later she, herself, was falling off to sleep in Susan Manus's bed, and the roar of the sea was in her ears, and the picture of a lone figure in a pitching, foam-crested curragh waa in her mind.

CHAPTER 29

The drifter went back. The storm still raged. Peggy Miley was well and so was the baby. The doctor was still on the island. He was over in the schoolmaster's. Ruth was at Manus O'Donnell's, and she spent the night in the kitchen with the men, who had collected round the fire as usual. The island, freed from the tension of the last few days, was light-hearted again.

But the long storm was telling on the island supplies. Baking soda was scarce; sugar was short, but it was the tobacco supply that worried the assembly in Manus's. Manus himself was smoking tea. Neil Rodgers grew a supply of tobacco for himself, and dried it on the hob at home. He, alone, however, could smoke it. Charlie Doogan was partial to a wild herb, but tea was the general substitute.

In the midst of a talk about wild days and great efforts, Neil Rodgers lit up a new pipeful. He was close to Manus. 'Arrah, damn on ye, Neil,' Manus protested, 'ye'd stink a nation. Ye'll poisin yerself: baste or man couldn't stand that stink.'

Neil took the pipe out of his mouth, and blew a ring of smoke towards Manus.

'There's not the bate of that in the country,' he enthused. 'There's some body to it: yerself an' yer tay. Better do like the childer an' smoke brown paper.'

'I thought Charlie Doogan's bruscan was bad, but yours is the daddy of all. I never smelt nothing like it. I'd smoke dry cow-dung before I'd touch it.'

Manus got to his feet and reached to the mantelpiece for the tea-box, but his spouse had a word to say.

'Come ye, boy,' she objected, 'leave back that box. Nice face ye'll have on ye in the mornin' if there's no tay. Here, give it to me: 'I'll give ye a pinch.'

'But he has me stinked sick,' Manus pleaded. 'Better take the pipe from him: he'll blacken yer walls, and the priest's comin' to the stations.'

Ruth's laugh from the room brought Manus's eye to her. He slapped his hand on the side of the kitchen bed. 'Come up an' sit here, cailin,' he said, 'but damn ye, Neil,' he added in dismay, 'ye'll smother her.'

'No, he won't,' Ruth laughed; 'I'm sure I'll like the whiff of home-grown stuff.'

'Little ye know about it,' Manus said. 'He went into his own byre smokin', an' a bullock fell in a dead faint.'

Ruth produced a box of cigarettes she had borrowed from the doctor. She passed it round. Manus gripped a cigarette in his teeth, the top of it just protruding beyond his whisker. 'Tell ye what,' he said eagerly, 'I'll put it in me pipe.'

'Deuce a taste I can get out of it much,' Neil Rodgers said.

'Taste?' Manus mocked; 'bitter aloes in all ye could taste after yer pipe. There's soot in me nose from yer reek.' Manus lighted the pipe and puffed hungrily. 'Ye'd be thinkin' life strange on the island?' he said, turning to Ruth, 'though, 'pon me sowl, ye're too fine a girl to let back to them towns. We'd educate ye up to the life fine. The way ye clouted through them waves was clippin': I'd be makin' up to ye meself, if I was as young as some of the boys. Best thing ye could do is settle down on the island: we'll get ye a brave lump of a lad, an' don't let the trouble there was the day to get a doctor frighten ye.'

'Mush, ploid on ye, Manus but yer clean gone! He's fair light in the head smokin' tay,' his wife pleaded, addressing Ruth. 'Ye're not to heed a word he says.'

'Mary there was a Crolly woman: she used to wear a hat, an' was a terrible toff when I married her,' Manus went on confidentially. 'She was that thin though, ye could near see through her. Lucky for her I went to a raffle in ould Seimidh Brian's.'

'I suppose she was frightened at the sea at first,' Neil Rodgers suggested innocently.

'Well, I'll tell ye,' Manus said, 'we had to put heather on the bottom of the boat before she'd come into it.'

'Don't you want to take a trip somewhere else at times?' Ruth asked, smiling at Mary Manus's wink.

'Take a trip somewhere?' Manus repeated. 'Faith no. I was out there in Traighenna a couple of winters, an' devil such a founderin' I ever got. Another summer I fished in Portnoo, I was near torn in flitters with fleas. Me sowl, no, I'm content to stay on the island here.'

'Oh, aye, it's a grand life,' a man with a slight Yankee accent put in; 'a grand life! smokin' tay on hungry bellies, out to yer waist in the tide slavin' after fish ye can't get – a grand life!'

'Plasham on ye,' Mary Manus retorted: 'yer couple of years away in 'Merica spoiled ye, to yer own way of talkin', but I don't see anybody so often stuck in a drain, or out to his backside in the tide as yerself. If it's all grand away from here, ye came back knowin' what there was here, an' seein' what the other was there, to live the hardest, slavinest life of the lot of us.'

'That's true for ye,' another commented. 'Mary here thinks

it's the like of ye puts the goin'-away idea into young fellows' minds. She'll guzzle ye dry yet on it.'

'I'll be for the States again, musha, but I must see me ould mother at rest first.'

'Ye're good to her. I'll admit that,' Mary Manus said. 'This is not a hard life, except that it may be a difficult place to make a living, with the sea, and storms, and the uncertain fishing. If one got pals with it all, it would be great,' Ruth said.

The Yank smiled pityingly. 'Get pals with hunger, an' pinchin', an' sparin', with never a halfpenny to bless yerself with. Oh, it's a grand life for a woman with a string of childer at her tail, an' her breasts weasened with hunger.'

'Chokin' to ye, Donal Hughie,' Mary Manus interrupted, her cheeks flaming, 'but it's the old woman's talk ye'd have on yer tongue. What d'ye know about rearin' a string of childer? An' who ever heard of a poor woman being dry-breasted? If there's a thing I hate it's a man full of old women's talk. Not but it's a hard place to rear childer,' she said, her anger, which was only embarrassment for Ruth, passing, 'an' when they're reared maybe, it's the sea reaches up an' takes them away,' she added, her thoughts on her drowned boy.

Donal Dubh got to his feet. 'It's a hard place to rear childer, an' it's a hard, unfortunate place for a child to be reared in.' Then he went out.

'There's more sense in what Donal says than anyone admits,' Neil Rodgers said. 'What chance has a child born on this island, except to go to the Lagan to be hired, or to Scotland to the pratie diggin'? In all me memory we turned out in this island, one shop-boy, Mickey Melly's son, the Hughie fellow; a Glasgow policeman – red Margaret's son, a big, easy lump of a lad he was – an' two monitors, that never got the length of being teachers. The island's only a nursery for foreign parts.'

'Ah, damn ye, ye won't leave any heart in the cailin here to settle in the island,' Manus objected. 'Ye're goin' out of seed. I never heard such thin-blooded talk in me life. It's the men the like of her'd breed ye'd want among ye.'
Charlie lifted the latch and came in.
'We've wan man left yet, anyway,' Manus said.
'The doctor's wantin' to go,' Charlie said, 'an' the wind's eased. There's a moon out now.'
On the beach, Charlie lifted Ruth in his arms, and waded with her through the surf to the boat.

CHAPTER 30

The new prosperity in the district quickened life for the people. During the feverish rushes in and out to the West Bay, boats made and lost reputations, and the groups on the quay and in the public-houses boasted and denied with vehemence. These discussions moved along the coast, and through the islands, provoking clashing opinions, as they travelled. The clash excited interest, which fished up half-forgotten stories of closely matched boats, and great races. The idea of a regatta suddenly stood out in the local mind, without anybody knowing or asking who had mooted it. With the rumour of the regatta came tidings of an incident at Burtonport. Mason, who was chief of the local coast-guards, had words with Dr. Wilson about the seamanship of the islanders. The doctor flung at him the story of Char-lie Doogan's actievement. The coastguard retorted by flash-ing a five-pound note under the doctor's nose.
'I'll bet you two to one I'll pull rings round him over a mile course,' he challenged.
'I'll take your bet,' the doctor said.
Talk of the regatta suddenly faded, and the match between Charlie Doogan and the coastguard became the topic. The

local merchants saw their chance, and clubbed together to get prizes, and a regatta, with a challenge race as a star feature, was speedily arranged.

The doctor told Ruth of his clash with the coastguard. She insisted on their going straight away to the island to consult Charlie. They found him helping Neil Rodgers to thatch. The doctor told the story, while Ruth kept her eyes on Charlie's face, smiling at his blush when the doctor mentioned the curragh fight. She saw the interest leap into his eyes when he was told of the challenge. Charlie didn't speak for a moment. A boat was passing across in front of the strand; Susan Manus was rowing.

'Well, I'll try it,' he said.

'You must win, Charlie,' Ruth said. 'I met his wife, and she got so on my nerves that we ended up with a thumping fine row. I could never stand her if you lose.'

'Well, I'll win,' Charlie rapped out, with unusual energy. Ruth stepped back in mock alarm. 'Don't snap the head off me,' she protested.

After a few minutes' light talk they separated. Charlie went back to work on Neil's house; the doctor and his sister went across to the boat.

'Strength and good-will might not have beaten the other's training, but the fire you have raised will. It was keen of you to mention Mrs. Mason. Ruth, you and that chap could blaze up easily.'

'My dear man, don't I know it,' Ruth agreed, taking his arm.

The curate, who had come to the island on a sick call, waved to them. He went out with them in their boat.

CHAPTER 31

The islanders had already been interested in the regatta.
The challenge that had been accepted in Charlie's name
raised their interest to excitement. Mason was unpopular
too, for he had secured a conviction against Jack Doney
for failing to report a cask of petrol that had been washed
ashore. Biddy Melly's was ahum with nightly discussions,
mainly concerned with the manner of celebrating the victory. The whole island was to turn out in a body, with
Manus O'Donnell leading.

Charlie Doogan induced his mother to promise to come to
the regatta. For years she had never, to his knowledge, been
to a day's sport, except one St. Patrick's Day when she
brought him to Dungloe, but then there was a mission in
the town, and she wanted one of the holy fathers to read
an office for Nellie. She refused at first, although it thrilled
her to have a thing like this discussed around the fireside.
'Ah, have sense, a mhic,' she said, 'regatta indeed! What in
the world would I be doin' at it?'

'Amn't I goin' to pull?'

'Ye are. Ye're losin' the wee sense ye had,' she said, smiling.

'An' amn't I pullin' against Mason?' Charlie persisted.

'Musha, bad scrant to the same Mason; he's a plague. I
didn't like him the first sight I saw of him, an' that was
before ever he caught Jack Doney,' she said.

'He says there's not a man in the Rosses can touch him
with two paddles.'

'They say he's powerful good. He'll crow terrible if he beats
you, Charlie, an' you the pick of the islands,' she deliberat-
ed.

'Who says that?' he asked.

''Tis, anybody with two eyes, God bless ye,' she said.

'I'm goin' to bate him. Come out an' I'll give ye the prize
money to spend.'

'Faith an' it's well I could spend it,' she replied, taking out her snuff-box. 'Where money goes is a fair caution. There's yerself now wantin' a pair of boots, an' Nabla's new coat is in tatters, an' the inspector comin'. We'll have to keep things terrible tight till we see how the kelp does, or we'll be back where we left.'

'Devil a back, mother,' he said, lighting his pipe. 'I'm thinkin' of burnin' shells an' makin' lime. I hear there's a great want of it outside.'

'Indeed I mind the time me father used to burn a couple of big kilns every year,' she said.

'Mary Manus is comin' to the regatta,' he told her.

'Oh, not a toe,' she protested.

'She is then, an' Manus too, an' Aunt Mary, an' Nappy Sheamuis, an' of course all the men.'

'It's because Neil is goin' that yer Aunt Mary is goin', for she knows fine he'll go on the tare. An' Mary Manus is goin' to keep Manus off the batter. Indeed wan way or another I'm thinkin' it's a rum island we'll have that night, if you win. Is Mason as good as they say, d'ye think? Be the post-boat's news yesterday, ye'd think he was a steam engine be himself.'

'I'll bate him,' Charlie assured her.

'If ye do, Charlie, or whether ye do or ye don't, don't let them put drink in ye; d'ye mind the night of the tailor's raffle? God bless us all, but ye put me in mind of yer father, when he'd taste a drop long ago. I saw him smashin' every plate on the dresser, an' leoga, he was the man that slaved hard to keep a house goin'. There's breeds of people an' drink drives them fair daft,' she warned.

'There's breeds of drink that fair drives any man daft,' he defended.

'That's true enough, be what I hear, but when you win the morrow all the island an' half the parish'll be for spillin' drink down yer throat,' she persisted.

'Come out then, an' I'll promise not to taste a drop. Now, that's a bargain. When were ye at a day's sport last?'

''Tis, the time long ago that the horse races was in Mahery. Yer father was ridin' a horse for Johndy Ban.'

'I never heard of that,' Charlie said.

'No, it was shortly after we were married. Faith, an' it's a brave race he made, for a bit. The poor baste was fed on weeds, an' while the weeds lasted he went like the wind. They say horses should be fed like christians for them races, with eggs an' everythin'. I promised I'd never go to a day of the kind again. We had most never to get home. Men never seem to see how much drinkin' spoils a day on the women. It's proud yer father'd be the day if God had spared him,' she said.

'Wasn't he the greatest oarsman in the island in his day?' Charlie asked.

'He was, but his day went down early. Nobody could have stood the way he went on anyway, never heedin' rain more'n it was sunshine.'

Mary Manus came strolling in, in the bare feet, knitting her sock. 'God save all here,' she said.

'Amen, an' you too.'

'I hear Manus is goin' to the regatta.'

'He is, an' devil all is under him an' Neil Rodgers but to go on the batter. This'll be the topsy-turviest island ever a livin' mortal saw, when Charlie bates Mason. Am goin' out meself, an' am tellin' Manus that I'll take every other glass with him, if he tastes.'

'Charlie here is at me to go out,' Mary Doogan said.

'An' why shouldn't ye? 'Deed, sowl, ye'd be the dry nature of a woman if ye didn't go out to see yer own son pull a race.'

'But who'll mind the house? Ye can never depend on childer; not an ounce wan of them wans has more'n the other.'

'Annie Patsy says she's not goin' to the regatta, but is waitin' for the dance. She's makin' a dress for Ellen Miley. The poor cratur hasn't a stitch. It's the aunt that was in last week that put in the makin's of the dress to her, an' as nice a shade of blue as ever ye set yer eye on. I wish I knew where she got it, an' what it cost, I'd get a length of it for Susan, in a better quality of stuff, maybe,' Mary Manus said.

'If Annie Pat was to keep an eye on the childer, I'd be content. I'll leave the hens' mate ready, an' all she'll have to do is to see that somebody keeps the ducks away; dirty gulpins of ducks, that I didn't get an egg out of since I don't know when.'

'Oh, Annie'll do that,' Mary Manus assured her. 'An' let us lave brave an' early in the mornin', an' make a day of it, when it's a thing we're goin' at all.'

'Musha, wagga, an' it's little notion I had of goin' to the regatta,' Mary Doogan said, putting her fingers into Mary Manus's snuff-box.

CHAPTER 32

The day of the regatta was one of sunshine and light breezes. Four boats left the island before noon. There were crowds of people promenading the quayside, where apple-women, thimble-men, three-card-trick men, Tom Laurence and his air-gun, wheedled their halfpence from them. A fortune-teller, assisted by a bird, that picked the summary of the inquirer's fate from thousands of leaflets, did a roaring trade. The sailing events came first, and closely contested by local crews, stirred excitement by their distributed partisans. Cheers and counter cheers rang out as a Gola boat cut in on an Arran boat or a Kincaslagh skipper passed a Mahery one. But the crowd settled down into one hum when the racing contest came on. Mason, the coastguard, stood forth as a challenger while Gola men and Arran men and mainland men alike had the desire for a local champion. Mason appeared in a blazer, a splendid type of aggressive, virile manhood. He took his seat in his cockleshell boat, and settled down to wait, running his eye over the crowd, provocatively self-assured.

The competing locals emerged from the clustered boats by the quayside, and took their allotted positions, big-boned, fair-faced youths, with no great determination stamped on their faces, rather amusement that had accepted defeat, and was already smiling away the failure.

Charlie Doogan was the last to go to the post. He was stripped to the waist. His face looked pale under his black hair. There was no trace of amusement on his face, but great concentration and strong purpose.

'I wonder has he his shirt in the boat with him,' his mother said to Mary Manus. 'There's some light-fingered gentry about this same port.'

'Most likely he left it back there with the doctor. I saw him with him before the race.'

'Musha, I don't know what tempted him to strip like that. But there's Mason throwin' off the thing he was wearin', an' he's stripped too. 'Declare him an' Charlie is noddin', an' what d'ye think, he's offerin' to shake hands.'

'Charlie shouldn't have shook his hand,' Mary Manus said. 'Maybe it's some poison that man would put in his hand that'd deaden it of a sudden.'

'Charlie's too trustin' that way. I hope it's in his own boat he has the shirt, for I put a patch on the right shoulder, an' I hadn't a bit of white thread in the house. I sewed it with black. I wouldn't for anythin' that anybody'd see it. Isn't it duncey the like of it happens? The young dog carries everythin' out, an' he lost the white spool on me.'

'Young dogs be like that,' Mary Manus said.

'They're gettin' ready,' Mary Doogan said. 'Isn't it a wonder they don't ali pull off their summits?"

It was Dr. Wilson who had induced Charlie to remove the

heavy undershirt. The doctor himself removed it indeed, and when Charlie suddenly found himself exposed, and Ruth in the group by the doctor, his face went scarlet.

She plucked the doctor. 'Isn't he a picture?' she said.

'Perfect. And he's a tiger for dash, I'll swear.'

'Give him back his shirt; he'll be too embarrassed.'

'It's your eye is fetching the blushes, Ruth.'

She didn't even smile. 'Why aren't men of that sort more common,' she asked, mostly to herself. 'If that fellow had a thousand a year, Dick, he'd be lionized. I'd be flinging myself at him.'

'If he flung himself penniless at you, Ruth, you'd be in danger. But Charlie is not likely to go after you unless you become a lobster.'

'I wonder,' Ruth said, almost to herself.

The moment for the start of the race came. Mason, his eye on the starter, crouched for a quick start; training was manifest in his wonderful concentration. All interest in the crowd was gone. His task absorbed him.

Charlie Doogan, too, crouched for a good start, but his concentration was less successful. Now and again his name was called from the shore, and his attention wandered.

'Hush, sh – sh – sh,' Dr. Wilson began. Silence fell. And then the signal was given. Mason and Doogan shot forward, the others followed like a scattered volley. Mason was slightly ahead. With a whirlwind of short, powerful strokes, he fought clear of the throng, heading unerringly for the flagboat. Charlie Doogan showered strokes that were not so rapid as Mason's, but left the water with a greater snap.

'Can he hope to keep that up?' the doctor murmured.

Ruth was silent.

Charlie drew level with Mason, drew slightly ahead. The crowd broke into one wild yell, and then silence.

'If I'd known of this I'd have made him swallow eggs,' Sally Doogan said, remembering the Mahery races.

Mason was first round the flagboat. The great crowd was silent. Then Charlie swept round and entered on the straight for home. It was a battle of evenly matched giants. Stroke on stroke they fought, Charlie winning by fire, more than by weight and power. He crept up along the other, Mason playing perfectly fair, and not seeking to cramp him in any way. He drew level and was tied there. Mason made a spurt, and got a shade ahead. Charlie met the challenge, stuck to his opponent, paying him stroke on stroke, heaving body in line with heaving body. Then he made his dash.

The two men were gasping, their bodies straining to breaking point, blood singing in their ears, sweat scalding their eyes. And then suddenly the fight snapped. Mason, swinging forward for a stroke, swayed, struck the water with one oar, recovered himself, struck an ineffective stroke, and then fainted.

Charlie swept by the winning post, amid the roar of the local population, and then swinging round, went back to his opponent, to whom the doctor was being rushed. He had recovered, and smiled up at Charlie, as he took the proffered hand.

'I am glad it was an islander beat me,' he said. 'I'm an islander myself.'

CHAPTER 33

Mary Doogan sat very quietly in her place when Charlie appeared round the flagboat; as he drew level with Mason she gripped Mary Manus's arm. When Mason collapsed she groaned, associating his collapse with the strain on Charlie. 'He's not fed for it, Mary, he's not fed for it,' she said.

'But he's bred for it,' Mary said, joining in the yelling.

'Did he win?' Mary Doogan said. 'Did our Charlie win?'

'Get to yer feet,' Mary said, 'he won. By the Lord, he won. There'll be a night in our island. Divil a stop 'll put on Manus for wan day.'

'Is it our Charlie everybody's cheerin'?' Mary Doogan asked, taking a grip of Mary Manus's arm again.

'To be sure it's Charlie. I wouldn't for a sovereign have missed that.'

'I never saw him coming in at all,' Mary Doogan said. 'I closed me eyes, I think, when the other man's oars went in the air. Did he faint?'

'He came to all right. Devil the much odds. He'll be a quiet boy for the future. This pricks his windbag.'

'Mary, ye're as daft as the rest. I near suffocated. An' the prize is our Charlie's! Well, a Dhia na gloire, think of that. I was sure of me life the bacon an' the eggs, the beef an' the fowl that other man ate would tell in the end. Not a thing poor Charlie ever had exceptin' dry bread an' tay, an' praties, an' herrin' an' sometimes he could be doin' with it oftener than he got it, for young people eat a dozen times in the day.'

'It's not the size of the gut but the pluck that counts. Come on an' we'll have tay for ourselves at one of them tay houses.'

'Arrah, for Heaven's sake, Mary, not a tay I'll have. They charge ye the three prices. I have the full o' me pocket o' dulsk.'

'Come on, Charlie's after winnin' the prize. We'll do somethin' we never done before, an' that's pay money for a drop o' tay.'

They made their way through the crowd, to where a large sign 'Refreshments' pointed out what they sought. Mary Manus led the way in.

'Did ye ever see so many feedin' at wan time, barrin' a gatherin', or a wake, God save us,' Mary Doogan said.

'Ye might have said a weddin',' Mary Manus replied. 'Here's a corner.'

They made their way to two vacant seats at the far end. 'Mind, would that old form give way with you,' Mary Doogan said. 'It's rickety enough for anythin'.'

''Clare to me goodness if that's not a nail,' Mary Manus said, rising and feeling with her hand. 'That'd fair tair the seat out of a man's trousers. Heigh, girl,' she called one of the waitresses.

She came up.

'Have ye a hammer?'

'A hammer?'

'Aye, a hammer: for that matter the shoulder of the tongs 'ud do. See that nail.'

'Well, can't ye keep away from it?'

'I can: I can keep away from it, but the next body mightn't keep away from it. We must hammer it down.'

'Let what doesn't concern ye alone.'

'What doesn't concern me! Troth me, lassie, it'll be well for the man gets ye. Ye'll be a savin' housekeeper. It's not fal-the-dals like them white ribbons ye'll be wearin', but the hem of yer skirt'll be up to yer houghs an' yer legs red with the ayre from the drab.'

'Maybe, if people saw yerself when yer potterin' about the house, it's the ashes bes on yer toes, an' the ABC on yer shins with toastin' them in the fire.'

'It's not the want of the gab'd be on ye. But I'll hammer the nail. I'll loose me shoe an' hammer with the heel. There's a half-tip on it: 'I'll swear an' yer a young girl, least yer not married yet – I'll swear ye couldn't dare take off yer shoe where ye stand for shame the way yer toes is stickin' miles out of yer stockings.'

The girl blushed, then she walked off indignantly. Mary took off her boot and hammered the nail.

'Did ye tear yer skirt, Mary?'

'I didn't; I planked straight down on top of it an' I got up straight. It's fine now. Where's she?' She waved to her.

'Hoigh!' she called.

A different girl came.

'We'll have two fine bowls of tay,' Mary Manus said.

'Cups ye mean,' the girl said, smiling.

'Cups I don't mean,' Mary said. 'Bowls I mean.'

'I'll slip out an' see can I get ye two bowls. I'm only in for the day. They try to be terrible polite here with cups an' forks, an' the devil knows what.' She went off.

'That's like a daughter of Paddy Andy's,' Mary Doogan said. 'She has their eyes an' their voice.'

'Troth, ye're right,' Mary Manus said. 'I was wonderin' who she was. The other wan's some droich I don't know.'

'She's not like any breed of people I know either,' Mary Doogan said. 'I wouldn't like her either. There's a hardness about her. A young girl that has no nature in her for a man's Sunday trousers is only a stacan. What at all time will we get home d'ye think?'

'I'm resigned to get in when I get in,' Mary Manus said. 'It's not every day we bring the best oarsman of the coast to the island. Mary Doogan, ye're the quarest woman in the world. It's kind of frightened ye are that he won. Ye'd think it's me was his mother.'

'He's the best son ever a poor woman reared,' Mary said, 'an' it's seldom I talk like that.'

'I hope he'll be a good son to more'n you. Biddy Melly tells me him an' our Susie's as thick as thieves. Susie has the snuggest place in the island, an' the warmest wee girl in the parish herself, an' it's not often I say it. Nothin'd please me better than to see that.'

'But Biddy says a lot,' Mary Doogan said.

'She does; but I was duking round the stacks wan night, an' I saw herself an' him comin' home from a ceilidh in Rosie's, an' I saw enough for meself. A body has to keep an odd eye out on their own.'

Mary Doogan sighed. 'Our day'll soon be over, Mary, an'

it'd be great to see the young wans facing life in right harness. An' I hope life doesn't be as hard for them as it was for some o' us.'

'Amen, musha. Anyway, this day looks like we were pushing ahead. Here she is, an' I declare she has two blue bowls. If there's one thing I like it's blue delph. An' a taypot all for ourselves too. You're a bully girl,' Mary Manus concluded.

'Are ye wan of the Paddy Andy's,' Mary Doogan asked.

'I am, Fanny's daughter,' the waitress said.

'Well, do you tell me; yer mother was the best quilter in the parish.'

'She quilts away yet.'

'Arrah, who made this tay?' Mary Manus demanded, interrupting the pouring.

''Tis I'll tell ye,' Fanny's daughter explained. 'I wet it just now mesel'. The heart is stewed out of what they have up there. Give it a minute.'

Mary Manus put a spoonful of sugar in the teapot and stirred it. 'That's all right now,' she commented, when she recommenced pouring.

They were charged a shilling each for the tea; each of them paid her own shilling.

'Well, a shilling for that,' Mary Doogan said when they got outside. 'That was Johndy's sixpenny loaves and we didn't ate apast two slices each; that wouldn't be twopence worth of bread, and that jam is only tenpence a pot; we didn't take the half of a haporth of jam between us. It's fair robbery.'

'What do ye expect at a regatta, only the like o' that?' Mary Manus said. 'Sure it's the only chance they get, God help them.'

'It's a poor way of makin' a livin', musha,' Mary Doogan said, 'makin' it out o' the bite that a body puts into her mouth. I'd rather scrape me nails off through the rocks than do the like o' it. Where are we headin' for now?'

"Tis I'll tell ye,' Mary Manus said. 'I wasn't up in Nora Nelly's since the youngster died. Not a better thing the two of us could do than drop up. Nora is the one that wouldn't be lame or lazy to make a trip herself, an' she never shuts her eyes to a body when she meets her out.'

'If we had thought we were goin' up to Nora's it's a pity we bothered at all about the tay,' Mary Doogan said.

'Arrah, damn on yer old shillin',' Mary Manus protested. 'Don't let hard ways stick to ye once you can help it, and with your risin' family round ye now ye've the tide broken.'

'It's aisy for ye talk, Mary Manus, with your money in the bank an' yer long purse under the pillow.'

'Aye, an' me wan boy's bones somewhere at the bottom of the Atlantic,' Mary Manus countered with a sigh.

'It was a heartbreak for ye to lose Hughie the duncey way you did, if it was God's will,' Mary Doogan said.

And they were both silent for awhile on their way up to Nora Nelly's.

CHAPTER 34

Charlie Doogan slipped away from the crowd down in Campbell's to run up to Doctor Wilson's. The doctor and Ruth had been on the slip when he had landed and tried to get him off with them. But ranged behind the doctor and waiting for Charlie to be free to join them were the Islanders. They were restraining Neil Rodgers and Phil Boyle until Charlie had finished with the strangers. It would be wrong of course for Charlie to go off with mainland people after winning a race, but he promised to go up later. There were many people present when Charlie was shown into the big room in the doctor's. Doctor Wilson sprang to his feet and led the cheer. Tea was being handed round just then, but it was interrupted for a toast. Afterwards Ruth herself continued taking round the tea. Charlie would gladly have escaped the ordeal of drinking tea in such strange surroundings. He tried to lift the cup off the saucer, but Ruth quietly resisted him. He smiled frankly at her as he collected himself. When he refused a second cup she didn't press him.

There was to be a dance and the whole roomful was going. Charlie explained that he would have to go back to the island first. Most of the islandmen were merry and would not go home without him. Ruth sat beside Charlie, a gramophone was set playing and there was besides a buzz of talk.

'You are a whopper,' Ruth enthused, when she and Charlie were alone on the sofa. 'It was the most exciting thing I've ever seen, it kept me gasping.'

'I was gaspin' meself when it was over,' Charlie said.

'I'm surprised you are not gasping yet; you looked fierce,' she added.

Charlie had never had himself discussed like this before; interest from such a girl as Ruth Wilson was embarrassing, but it was pleasant.

'I was afraid of what 'ud happen if I lost,' he said. 'I didn't want Mason's wife crowin' o'er you.'

Ruth laughed. 'As a matter of fact, Mason's wife is a poor little mouse of a creature that wouldn't crow over anybody. I made up that part of the story,' she said. 'Wasn't that wise of me?'

He nodded, and he didn't smile.

'You'll be at the dance?' she asked.

'I will.'

They were both silent during a short lull in the conversation. Then Charlie laughed, not loudly but a bit harshly.

'Well, what is it?' Ruth asked.

'Had the doctor his bet on itself?' he asked.

'The doctor? Of course he had. Why do you ask?'

'Why did you tell the other story?' he asked her, searching her with his grey blue eyes.

She was embarrassed.

'I wanted you to win,' she said simply. 'It just blurted out, and afterwards I wanted to feel you thought you were rowing with that bet in it.'

'There wouldn't be much in winnin' a race unless it was for something. I have a feeling now there was no race at all; none as far as my mind goes.'

'Oh, but there was,' she insisted. 'You took up a challenge –'

'I didn't; I only backed them that took it up. Myself, I wouldn't have taken it up.'

'Are you sorry now you rowed?' she asked.

'I'm not so glad as I was,' he said.

The local D.I. came over and sat on the seat beside them. He was full of Charlie's great feat and inclined to be patronizing.

'Why in the world is a splendid chap like you remaining stuck away on an island? Don't you get awfully bored and sick of it at times?'

'It might come to that,' Charlie agreed, 'though I never thought of it before.'

'The police force would give a grand opening to a young man like you,' the D.I. continued. 'If I could help in any way, of course I would be only too glad. Miss Wilson here is such a friend of yours –'

Charlie interrupted the D.I. with a laugh.

'They'd put me in a sack an' drown me if they heard on the island that I was joinin' the police,' he said. 'I'll stick to the sea.'

Then he got up to go home.

He promised the doctor he would drop up the next day he was in the Port.

Ruth saw him to the gate and neither spoke during the short walk down the avenue.

'You are angry, I think,' she said.

'I'm not angry,' he assured her, placing a hand on the gate. 'It reminds me of wan time I got a haul o' trout,' he continued. 'It seemed a great thing at first and then it got very small suddenly.'

'I asked you to win, Charlie, because I wanted you to win, because it gave me the greatest joy to have you win,' she said vehemently.

He faced her. The moon was shining on her upturned face. And it was the same look was in her eyes as when he carried her through the surf to the boat on the island strand. He pulled open the gate and to her half whispered, 'You will be at the dance?' he only nodded.

CHAPTER 35

Charlie and the women folk collected the islandmen and coaxed them to the boats. Manus was only merry; Neil Rogers was boisterous, Phil Boyle was impossible. It took both Susan Manus and Charlie to get Phil down to the quay. Only a few of the young folk and that few men went back to the island; they would return once they had seen the old folk safely home. All the others were remaining for the dance.

Charlie Doogan was delayed for a long time with Phil Boyle. Phil always became violent when he drank whiskey, and only Charlie could control him. It was past midnight before he went off to sleep. Charlie took a punt and set off at once for the Port.

It was a calm night with a shower of stars, a haze and a flood tide. The dance was strong in Charlie's mind. As he thought of it the dance narrowed its significance and he found himself worrying whether Ruth Wilson might not have gone by the time he reached. Ruth's face formed in the whirling waters in the wake of the punt; a pale,

earnest face. Stars glistened in the water, the face formed
about the brightest and eyes looked up into his.

'I'm not drunk,' he muttered, 'just daft.' He threw his
weight on the paddles and his buoyancy returned. The
silence of the night, the grey lonely mists on the water were
removed from him by the urge of his impatience.

He tied the boat hastily at the slip, and hurried up the
quay. He could see the lights in the dance hall. He heard
the tramp of the dancers. He pushed his way through the
groups outside the door. The warm stuffy air of the dance-
room struck him as he entered. A dance was in progress,
the second figure in a set of quadrilles. He joined the loose
throng inside the door. He had a good view of the house
over the head of the dancers.

People were leaving already. He became interested in a
movement along the wall where a group was pushing past
behind the dancers. He had a passing glimpse of the girl.
It was Ruth Wilson; soon she came clearly into view. She
was going home and the D.I. was walking in front making
way for her. When she was still a good distance from the
door she met Charlie's eye. She didn't smile, but just looked
at him gravely.

'I only just got back,' he said to her. 'I had to put a drunk
man to sleep.'

She was sorry now she had decided to go home. It was nearly
two o' clock, and she had not been particularly interested
in the dance. She had admitted frankly to herself that she
regretted, even resented, Charlie's absence. The resentment
settled into disappointment. To go back now after having
said good night to all the others, and having accepted the
D.I.'s escort, would be to give her change of mind too much
significance. She was still delaying beside Charlie when
there was a sudden surge forward from a corner of the hall;
regatta night dances are often disturbed. The crowd pushed
Charlie up against Ruth, crushing him against her. He put

his arms round her, and lifted her off the floor for a moment. Her hair was pressed against his face as he stooped over her. Then, releasing her, he threw out his arms, and putting all his strength into the jerk threw the crowd back, and as they gave way behind him, he saw her go out of the door with the D.I. hurrying her through the cleared space. Charlie didn't dance. He talked to a few of the island folk, and they told him that Susan Manus had gone up with one of Nora Nelly's daughters for tea. He didn't follow her there. He went slowly down the quay to where his punt was hanging alongside the slip. Then he entered his boat, and pushed off from the shore. There was no eagerness about his rowing. The sense of littleness had now soured into bitterness, as he crept out to sea under the starry heavens. He was disappointed. Life had ·suddenly become very empty. Unconsciously, he put weight on the paddles, and swirling water showed white in the boat's wake. And again there was that face! Sudden anger provoked a spurt of rowing. What a damn fool he was to let his thoughts stray in that way? What would put Ruth Wilson in his mind? Would she slave on an island? Would she starve on an island like his mother? He laughed, the bitterest laugh of life, the laugh of the man who mocks himself. Yet again came the face. Viciously he taunted himself, holding the picture of her as she passed round the tea that evening, and calling up the vision of island life. Her face faded, and the picture of the island remained. It was a sapless life, without joy, without hope. He thought of home, and Susan Manus came into his mind. For a moment he thought of Susan at the dance, and gave a passing thought to what the young folk would think of his going home by himself. Then the picture of the island life came back. It was a mean, hard life. He pulled savagely at the oars, and then suddenly he stopped. He thought of Nellie.

Nellie! Brassy! Brassy was the man who had caused Nellie's

death. He had vowed to go after Brassy. He had a promise of work at the new chapel at Raphoe, where a Crolly man was contractor. He would go after Brassy. His rage against Brassy suddenly caught fire. He wondered why he had remained at home so long. Impatience again hammered at him, as he swept across the water.

He told his mother simply that he was getting a job on the new chapel at Raphoe, and that he had to go at once. He told her to wire to him as soon as any herring fishing turned up. Raphoe was only a name to Mary Doogan. She only knew it was in Ireland, and didn't associate it with the Lagan or Brassy. She had often feared Charlie would go to Scotland, so that the announcement, while not welcome, was not as bad as it might have been. She didn't resist his going, but packed up his socks, and his shirts, and a pair of working trousers into an old oilskin coat, and tied it up for him. And just like the morning that Sally and Nellie left for the Lagan, she stood at the gable of the byre until the boat rounded the Point.

CHAPTER 36

Charlie Doogan's going away so suddenly took the heart out of his victory for the island. The old folks asked many questions to make sure he had not been drunk. The boys and girls exchanged confidences concerning the dance. Annie Patsy ventured the opinion that Charlie believed Susan Manus was out with some one else and that the story of her going for tea to Mary Manus's cousin was not accepted. Phil Boyle laughed that suggestion aside, and his knowledge of Charlie was the closest of anyone on the island, except perhaps Susan herself.

Susan gave no opinion. She could not define her own feelings towards the whole thing. Charlie and she had not

been the same pals for a long time. There was no good
reason, but they had not met so much nor were they as
easy with each other as had been the case before. What
Susan thought she kept to herself and her thoughts came
very near the truth.

Sally Doogan had been in the Port at the regatta and had
not returned for two days; she went over to Gweedore for
knitting and stayed a night in Crolly with Mary Manus's
people. It was Sally put the island minds at rest. She alone
knew where Raphoe was. She told them that Charlie had
sworn to get his five fingers on Brassy. Sally's story brought
no peace to Mary Doogan's mind.

Mary kept tight fingers on the few pounds they had still put
by after the fishing when most of their debts had been
plaid. Sally and she worked hard at the knitting; the other
children were kept busy on Carragheen moss and winkles.
Hughie made a small burning of kelp too.

'Keep the wee gains we have until another few years are
over our heads and the danger will be passed,' the mother said often, when urging the children to work.

Charlie wrote after a fortnight. It was a short letter, telling them he was well and working, and to tell Neil Rodgers that he was making coverings for lobster-pots in his
spare time. In Biddy Melly's, Susan Manus and Phil Boyle
met nearly every night. Often they went home together,
but Susan never told Phil what she suspected about Charlie,
and Phil never went further with Susan than the gap that
opened the near way to his home. A featureless three
months passed. Jack Doney was venturing out again and
had courage now to come an odd night to Biddy Melly's.
Mary Doogan took her knitting now and again and went
over to Mary Manus's or Mary Neil's a ceididh, Sally taking
charge round the fire in her absence. Whenever she went
like that to Manus's, Susan would go over to Sally, and
they would talk about Brassy and the threat Charlie had

made. In the end Susan found herself doubting her own early opinion.

'But still Charlie never wrote me,' she would say to herself when she found her belief in Sally's story growing.

And then suddenly Charlie came back. It was in the middle of the night he came, landing without warning under Manus's. He was not alone. A man from the Lagan district was with him, a man that was wanted by the police and had a price on his head. The man had befriended Charlie on the fair day that he had got his fingers on Brassy; he had headed the rush that drove back an attempt to hold Charlie for the police. Next day Brassy refused to make any charge against his assailant, and not a word could the police get out of him though they called daily on him during the six weeks he was in hospital.

Charlie brought the wanted man to Manus's. It was the only house on the island with a spare room; besides, the Manus's were a people with a reputation for being that way of thinking. When Charlie knocked Susan was the first to know it was he. Mary Manus herself hopped out of bed when the dog barked, and when she heard Charlie's voice at the door she glanced down at Susan's bedroom. It was the time of the year when a man calling at that hour where there was a marriageable girl, had a meaning.

Mary Manus welcomed Charlie, and welcomed the stranger. Then she lit the lamp. Manus called Charlie over to the bed and told him it was a sight for sore eyes to see him. Just then Susan came up from the room in the bare feet. Her cheeks were flushed and she welcomed Charlie warmly. Charlie told them about the stranger and how the police were after him. Susan put a heavy shawl on the window to hide the light and while the kettle was boiling they sat round the fire and discussed the situation. Manus was overjoyed to shelter the man that was 'on' his keeping'; Mary Manus pitied his mother; Susan was intensely interested in himself. Up to then she had seen men fight the sea and the storm, and such a fight might frighten or awe, but it did not thrill in this way. She had seen drunk men fight, but then her only feeling had been to be anxious to see the fight stopped. But this was something new. It was not only new to her experience but to her thoughts. And the stranger himself was arresting. He was not so tall as Charlie; he was lightly built. He talked rapidly and well, laughed lightly over his danger. And he was good-looking. His name was Friel. Susan was excited.

It was decided that the stranger would live in the spare room. At night very great care would be taken that the light didn't shine through the window. It would be given out that the gable was getting damp and that would account for the fire, for a while anyway.

'If Biddy Melly sees a gleam of light out of that window she'll know something is afoot,' Manus said. 'Ye'll have to mind the light.'

'I'll do that,' Susan said decidedly.

Later when Charlie got up to go home, Susan was sitting in the corner opposite the stranger and drinking in the story he was telling.

Mary Doogan had the happiest surprise of her life when Charlie's voice roused her that morning.

CHAPTER 37

Charlie Doogan and Phil Boyle spent as much time as they could about Manus's, though for appearance sake they made a nightly visit to Biddy Melly's.

Susan Manus gave Friel his meals. She saw to it that he had plenty of turf on the fire. They told Biddy Melly that the gable was going damp, and failed to notice Biddy's anxiety to examine it.

By and by Susan got to sitting by the fire on and off talking to the stranger. They had many smothered laughs together. He told Susan that Charlie had hammered Brassy, but he gave no details. It was a mercy he didn't kill him, was all he said. She asked Charlie about it, and he told her that Friel saved him from a crowd of Orangemen. It was before Friel went on the run. He might not have come home so soon only Friel was being closely hunted.

One evening Susan had put turf on the fire and was standing beside Friel, where he leaned against the mantelpiece. Strange voices sounded in the kitchen. It was mainland crew looking in for carrigan moss, the strange voices startled Susan, and she clasped Sean Friel's arm. For a few moments she held it until the conversation in the kitchen made itself clear to her. When she tried to release her hand Friel held on.

'Does me being here keep ye nervous that way?'

'I'd be frightened for them to get ye,' she said simply.

After that she didn't spend so much time with Friel, and had very little to say when with him.

That very evening there was a message with the post-boat for Charlie. The doctor's sister wanted to see him. He went out at once.

She was alone in the house when he called. She was baking and her hands were covered with flour.

'Shake my arm,' she said, extending an arm that was bare to the shoulder.

He shook it.

'So you're back,' she said, motioning him to a chair.

'I'm back,' he said, blushing slightly.

'You went away very suddenly,' she said, bending over the scones. He didn't speak.

'Why did you go?'

'Sometimes a man does a thing without asking himself a lot of questions.'

She turned to face him. 'Was it because of me?' she challenged.

'It was,' he said, sitting up straight in his chair. Then he got to his feet. 'Ruth Wilson, what did ye want with me?' It was an appeal more than a demand. It had a touch of reproof in it. He knew little of the ways of women, and saw nothing of the feeling in her face as she stood there. After a moment she shut her eyes and turned away.

'Why did you come back?' she asked.

'I had a reason for coming back,' he said gruffly.

'You came the morning after Billy White was shot,' she said. 'You didn't come by train. Maybe you didn't come alone.'

It did not occur to him she might be seeking knowledge. 'What have you to tell me?' he asked her.

'To-morrow morning about dawn the island will be raided.' He took an impulsive step towards her. He laid a hand on her shoulder. 'You're great,' he said simply.

She smiled up at him.

'I must be off now,' he said, putting on his hat.

'And you – are you going away too?'

'I'm not. There's a lot to be done at home.' And then he went out.

She sighed as she turned to put away the bread dish.

When it got dark that night Sean Friel slipped down to the shore. Charlie and Phil waited with the boat. Susan brought him to the spot. She murmured her farewell, and stood on a rock until the boat sank into the bank of grey mist.

They landed Friel, and brought him to a friendly house. He promised to return to the island now and then, and they arranged how he could send word. The people they left him with were friends of Phil Boyle's folk, and no heed would be given to one of them going into the island.

It was late when they got back to the island, and Charlie

went across the sandbanks home. He didn't know that Susan Manus was kneeling at the window to hear his step, so that she might know they hadn't run into the police.

Next morning Charlie woke to hear footsteps round about the house. He heard the steps passing the window. He chuckled to himself. Then came the tap at the door. He was sorry he hadn't given his mother a hint. The sight of policemen would scare her. He heard the steps on the kitchen floor, and the voices.

'Don't worry yerself now,' the sergeant was saying, 'we're not lookin' for any islander. We want a stranger, an' we want a word with your Charlie.'

'What under God d'ye want with Charlie?' she asked.

'Nothin' much: just to ask him a question or two. We must go through the house, ma'am,' he added.

'Ye're awake,' the sergeant said to Charlie.

'I'm not wan of the seven sleepers, an' ye've been goin' like a foghorn.'

'Is there another regatta comin' on? What brought ye back?'

'I saw in the *Journal* where they got herrin' at Kincaslagh.' The sergeant nodded. He read the *Journal* himself. 'An' why didn't ye come be train?'

"Tis, I got on to a fellow goin' to Glenties, an' he gave me a lift to Doohery,' Charlie lied.

'Go back to yer sleep,' the sergeant said. 'I knew we were on a fool's errand.'

Charlie dressed and went outside. Groups of police and military were scattered over the island. Biddy Melly was outside in the bare feet. She ran over to Charlie.

'Did they get him?' she asked breathlessly.

'Who was there to get?'

'Whist man: in Manus's. I was puttin' in the ducks the other night; I saw a thread of light comin' out of the window; I made an excuse into the house, an' the room-door was shut. Manus wasn't in the kitchen, an' what on earth ever took Manus to the room? Then last Tuesday didn't I see Mary Manus gettin' eight ounces of tobacco. What'd Manus be doin' with that much? I think I'll slip over to Manus's.'

'Ah, for Heaven's sake go back to yer bed, an' don't let yer tongue drag ye into trouble. Were ye talkin' to the police?' he concluded sharply.

'Ah, now, maybe I know as well as yerself when to talk.' He watched Biddy go back home. He saw Susan Manus come out to the gable. He raised his right hand in greeting. She started to come across and he hurried to meet her.

'Under God, Charlie, did he get away, or are they all over the place outside too, d'ye think?'

'He got away,' Charlie said, and told her where they had left him. Then to lighten the strain he told her about Biddy Melly.

Susan went back home in a happier mood, a little proud of the man whom so great a force hunted.

CHAPTER 38

At breakfast the morning of the police raid Charlie Doogan suddenly realized that his mother looked ill. She was more worn and thin than she had ever appeared. He felt a new tenderness towards her. Her talk revealed the worry his time in Raphoe had caused her. He was not sorry for hammering Brassy, but he was more honest with himself now as to why he went.

'You'll have to see the doctor,' he said to her, after dinner. She was secretly pleased that he should fuss over her, though she pooh-poohed the idea of a doctor. 'Anyway,' she concluded, 'God has been very good to me. Look at the change in the last twelve months; I don't hear anyone cryin' of hunger now. I'd rather die when ye're all around me, if it was God's will.'

Then Charlie went out to his work. Mary Doogan was feeding the hens at the corner of the gable, running her eye over them, speculating on whether this one would soon be laying, or whether another was due to moult. One dapper hen with shiny back she shook her fist at.

'Ye dodged me yesterday, me lady,' she said. 'Maybe ye're not the only wan's layin' out. I'll watch ye the day.'

She took out her stocking and sat on a flag knitting.

'Sally!' she called. 'Hoigh, Sally!'

Sally came to the door. 'Well?'

'Watch for fear the side of the pot'd get red. Better take out the praties an' leave them on the edge of the ashes.'

Sally disappeared.

The hens were breaking up and scattering over the street. The dapper one looked sideways, with an eye half shut at the woman on the flag.

'Hoigh, Sally!'

'Well, now?'

'I see the childer gettin' out, leastways I see the girl goin' over for the master's lunch. They'll be out in a minute. Ye'll get onions in the can that's hangin' at the end of the dresser.'

The dapper hen was moving down the lawn, making a pretence of pecking at shells. Mary pretended not to see, but she smiled to herself.

'If she bates me the day I'll say no more.'

The hen went on, moving over towards the potato field. Mary got to her feet, and walked across the green, knitting as she walked. This hen had been laying out and had baffled Mary's attempts to locate her nest. This was to be a great test.

The hen turned back casually, Mary went unheedingly on, out through a gap and into a neighbour field, and then round to take her place on an untilled shallow spot in the potato field. She could still see the hen. She folded her stocking; the click of the needles would be heard. Presently the hen looked carefully round, seeing the way clear she ran in among the potato tops. Mary lay down on her face, so that she could see the movements among the drills. Coming towards her too, the hen was, coming freely, almost hurriedly. Mary shut her eyes the hen halted, and held her breath. Looking through half-opened lashes, she saw the hen come slowly on, stepping high like a person tiptoeing and wishing to keep from rustling long grass. Mary tried to remain still, but she must have lowered her head slightly, for a blade of grass tickled her nose. She shook her head involuntarily. The hen halted and then let out a great cackle. Mary sat up. She knew her attempt had failed. She determined to frighten the hen, and perhaps ease her feelings. She stooped for clods. She saw a small piece of stick that could be thrown easily; she stretched out her hand, and just then her eye caught sight of white, round – eggs; the lost nest. She laughed. She stood up and looked after the cackling hen.

'It's my laugh, me lady,' she said. 'It's my laugh. Ye're caught,' and she laughed, but the hen ran on.

Mary gathered the eggs into her apron, eight of them, and turned home. She was happy in her mind. The crops were looking well. Kelp was a good price, and they had a good kiln ready, and Charlie was back. She sighed. She felt a dizziness; she staggered and put the free hand to her forehead. The dizziness passed, but a queer weakness remained. Her knees wobbled. She sat down for a minute. She got to her feet, but her head was spinning. She stooped to put the eggs safely on the ground. She stood up, but darkness was gathering round her.

'I must mind the eggs,' she murmered, as she fell sideways in a faint.

Neil Rodgers was cutting hook-grass, in the grassy drains of the cornfield. He saw Mary falling and rushed to her.

'Mary, God bless us, Mary.' He raised her to her feet. She moistened her lips with her tongue.

'I'll be all right in a minute. Mind them eggs.'

He put an arm round her shoulders. 'Lean on me,' he said.

'Amn't I the quare wan to be staggerin' like this,' she said. 'I'll walk,' she added, bravely attempting to overcome her weakness.

But her strength failed her, and before they reached the door he was practically carrying her. She was put to bed at once, and Sally raced over to the kelp kiln for Charlie. He was breathless when he reached the bedside. He looked at her for a moment before she opened her eyes.

'I took weak, Charlie, like happened me before.'

Mary Manus came in. She tapped Charlie on the shoulder. 'Go ye, at once for the priest. I don't like her at all.'

Charlie went out. He saw Phil Boyle going to the bog, and he waved to him. In a few minutes four men were driving a boat across the smooth water to the Port, four silent men rowing hard.

CHAPTER 39

Word went round that the priest was coming to Mary Doogan. Susan Manus came over to help her mother in getting the house ready. Maire Neil Rodgers was there before her. Mary Manus took down the curtains on the kitchen bed, and sent Susan over for the curtains on a bed in their room to put up in their place. Sally got busy washing up the delph, and fixing the dresser. The nets at the end of the house were again put on the loft in the barn. A small table with a spotless cloth, and clean white towel for the priest were wanted. Sally showed a new towel she had in the press, and the tablecloth that had been used at Nellie's wake on the table by the bed. There had been a hole burned in it, but Sally herself had patched it neatly. The woman spread it on the table. Maire Rodgers sent a child over to her house for a clean tablecloth that was in the corner of the press, one that she herself had embroidered. But it was too big. It would drop on the floor. It suited their table all right; perhaps it would be better to take over their table. But Mary Manus pointed out that the basin of water could be left on the table and oatmeal that is used instead of soap would be on plate; the basin would cover the patch, and the plate could be set on the little spot of ironmould. And all the time they worked and talked, they kept an eye on the bed where Mary Doogan lay, breathing softly.

Her only brother came and stood at the foot of the bed gazing at her. 'I don't like how she is at all,' he said to Mary Manus.

'Nor me,' Mary said thoughtfully.

She plucked Susan's sleeve. 'Run over, a chailleach, and get the blessed candle out of the drawer of the cupboard. It's wrapped up in butter paper: it's in the far corner. Run now.'

Susan ran over for the blessed candle. 'How is she?' Manus asked.

'Me mother sent me over for the blessed candle.'

The old man blessed himself.

Susan came back and left the candle on the table. 'It's as well to be prepared anyway,' she whispered to Maire Rodgers.

The other agreed.

The woman in the bed gasped, slightly, and raised her fingers to the edge of the clothes, and began toying with the quilt. Mary Manus and Maire Rodgers looked at each other, and shook their heads. The brother sighed.

'It'd be no harm to say the rosary,' Mary Manus said.

A youngster who had just come to the door ran across to a few houses. 'They're sayin' the rosary over Mary Doogan,' he said, and children were sent on to other houses. Soon the greater part of the island was gathered saying the fifteen decades for Mary. Towards the end she rallied, and joined in the prayers until the completion of the rosary.

'Sit there an' keep an eye on her,' Mary Manus said to the brother.

He sat by the bed. The quilt had raised up to her lips, and he carefully tucked it under her chin. He laid his horny hand on her forehead. She turned and saw him sitting there. 'Did anybody take in the eggs?' she asked. 'That dog of Neddy's 'll get them if not.'

'They're in,' he said.

'That's right,' she said. There was silence for a time.

'How're ye now?' he asked when she looked his way.

'All tired somehow,' she said. 'Tell Sally look out, maybe the ducks is at the hens' mate.'

He paled. She was raving. Only a few hours ago she had fed the hens herself, and had sat on the flag to keep away the ducks. He had seen her, but he sought to humour her. 'Sally's watchin'.'

'What was I sayin'?' she said, struggling to concentrate. 'Sure I saw the hens finish their feed meself. Don't let the black cow get a shower of rain,' she continued after a pause, 'an' it her first day out. An' it must be time to give the calf his drink.'

'It's near it. The calf'll be all right.'

'That's good,' she said, and sighed contentedly.

When the boat was seen returning Mary Manus spoke to her. 'How d'ye think ye are now, Mary?'

'I'm very weak.'

'Maybe ye might as well have the priest,' she said.

'He'll be welcome,' Mary said. 'It's only good he can do.

Maybe me work is o'er, Mary. Well, welcome be the will of God. I can leave them now easier. Gather them all round me, Mary, a chailleach.' Then she seemed to pass into a slumber.

The priest arrived. He anointed Mary and prepared her for death.

'What d'ye think of her, father?' Charlie asked.

'It's only a matter of hours. She's done.'

'God help us,' he said.

'Would a doctor be any use?' Charlie continued.

'Not a bit,' he said.

Charlie closed and opened his first, but didn't speak. He remained behind while the priest was rowed back. He leaned on a rail at the foot of the bed, gazing up at his mother. She called him. He went up and bent over her.

'Yon flour, Charlie?'

'I paid for it, first week of the herrin'.'

'That's good, Charlie, that's good. Ye'll help Sally look after them,' she said after a pause.

'I will, mother.'

'Gather them all round me.' The children were gathered round the bed. Her hand sought Hughie's.

A second rosary was begun. Charlie was leaning over her; her breathing was laboured.

'Don't cry a croidhe,' he heard her say. 'What can Ma do? Ye'll get tay – the morrow.' Then he heard her attempting to join in the prayers. 'God bless Charlie, poor mother never reared a better son.'

Charlie broke down, and left the bedside to Maire Rodgers. She began saying the prayers for a happy death into the ear of the dying woman. The brother's hand closed round the feelingless fingers that held the blessed candle, and she died that way.

Mary Manus closed her lips, and put a prayer book under her chin to keep the mouth shut, and then they all cried.

CHAPTER 40

After the burial of Mary Doogan, Charlie and Sally settled down to the task of rearing their younger brothers and sisters. Sally was as frugal as the mother. She kept a careful eye on the food supplies, saw that the ducks and hens were closed in at night, that clothes were mended, and she appealed to Charlie to enforce discipline when necessary.

Hughie had been in the mother's counsels, and he remained with Sally and Charlie. He had grown rapidly in the last year, and was becoming robust. Once Hughie was able to take on the farm work, and to take Charlie's place in Neil's boat, Charlie would go to Scotland. He would earn his passage to America, besides helping them at home. Once in America he would sent the passage money to the others as they grew up.

And Sally, poor Sally, she would remain to mother the brood, and by the time that was done her youth would be gone. She faced her task without thinking. Such was her stock and their code.

Ruth Wilson called at Doogan's after the mother's death. Charlie was out. She sat and talked with Sally. She found out their plans for the future, and when going away surprised Sally by giving her a friendly hug. Afterwards she wrote to Charlie. He got her letter when coming from a lagh strand. Sally was with him. She was walking in front, her wet petticoats flapping against her legs. The letter was just a short message of sympathy.

Charlie was very anxious to keep away from Ruth Wilson. He plunged into general work, fishing long lines, and pocket nets, early and late. Thoughts of his mother's death settled peacefully in his mind. The sense of loneliness remained when they were round the fire, and her name came up in a thousand and one ways, but the light-heartedness of the young soon filled the Doogan kitchen with laughter again;

occasionally Charlie's voice was raised in anger when he exercised his authority over the young folk.

Neighbours noticed how understanding Charlie was where help was scarce, how he often gave a few hours of an evening to assist families who were behind with their work. It was natural now that Charlie should not go near Biddy Melly's so much, and that gave him an excuse for spending nights in Manus's. He and Phil often smuggled Friel out and in. There was great trouble going on the mainland, and Manus was excited over the comings and goings of a man that was so much wanted by the police as Friel. So, indeed, were Phil and Charlie. They took very great delight over the stories the stranger told, when only themselves and Manus's family were with him round the fire.

'Tell me this,' Manus said to Friel one night, 'I heard that wee Phil Betty was took up an' tried for givin' information. It was Biddy Melly got the news someway. I heard it from others too. He was a terrible Hibernian, but his stock was as solid as that back stone.'

'He was taken up for writing a letter to a publican in Letterkenny; the publican was a bad lot. Inside was a lot of names of men that he said burned the Hibernian Hall. The letter was caught in a raid.'

'Well, damn!'

'We lifted Phil Betty: he maintained he only gave the names of five blackguards that wanted manners put on them, an' that the publican was the district secretary for his order.' Sean Friel laughed. The memory of the arrest amused him yet. Manus waited for the story. 'The courtmartial was funny,' Friel continued. 'The man is as full of national feeling as me, but he hadn't got on to the new way of expressing it.'

'Did ye ever hear of Mitchel?' said I.

'Mitchel,' says he. 'Who was Mitchel? Never heard of a man of the name round here.'

'Nor here,' Manus said, puckering his brows.

'He was a great Irishman that the English deported,' Friel explained, after a pause. The story was not so easy to tell; he didn't want the joke to be against Manus too.

'Ah, cripes!' Manus said, slapping his thigh, 'an' Phil thought it's some man from round about ye meant? Well, that's a good wan.'

Friel nodded. Susan laughed softly.

'Did ye ever hear what Tone set out to do?' says I.

'D'ye mane Toner?' said Phil Betty. 'There was a family be the name of Toner up the glen, an' wan of them was a bit of a fightin' warrior.'

'An' was Tone another of the ould warriors?' Manus asked.

'He was,' Susan said.

'Ah, well, that's the best ever – a man be the name of Toner –' Manus leaned on his stick to laugh. 'An' what happened then?' he asked, struggling with a cough.

'Would you like to see Ireland free?' says I.

'Would I what?' says he. 'Wasn't I a Home Ruler since the first day I mind?'

'He was, be heaventers,' Manus said. 'He was that. They were sound stock that way. I was in Letterkenny meself the day Cannon McFadden was tried, an' 'clare to me heavens if the Glen band didn't play the "Wearin' o' the Green" right up into the bayonets of the soldiers. Oh, damn the word lie. An' there was me bould wee Phil Betty batin' the triangle, an' nothin' would do him when the band was stuck, but to come up an' hit it under the very nose of the officer. Oh, fair's fair, wee Phil Betty was a man. But what happened next?'

'What'd ye do,' says I, to him, 'if wan of them fellows that's blowin' up police barracks up the country was to come to ye 'for shelter? An' then I saw I had hurt him. He stepped back an' he gasped –'

'What'd I do? Under God, what a question – Wouldn't I give him me heart's blood, if necessary?'

'He would then,' Manus said. 'The breed of him's sound.'

'Then we had a talk an' he went home at peace with us all. So anybody says anythin' against wee Phil Betty, ye can give them the lie.'

'Me sowl, an' I'm glad to hear that.'

Charlie and Phil got up to go. Charlie turned away home after a short 'so long.' Phil stood for a moment as though hesitating to call him back. Then he went slowly homewards.

CHAPTER 41

After months of wild rumours and great doings word came that the troubles on the mainland were ended, and that hunted men could walk about openly.

After a few weeks Sean Friel came back to the island and strolled about with Susan Manus. It is true that walking with Susan that way didn't prove anything since he was staying at Manus's, and there hadn't been any dance to show whether he would do Charlie out of leaving Susan home. But people began to notice how little Susan and Charlie were together. A dance was coming off in the school, and that evening a rumour got round among the young folk that Susan and Friel were to be married. Phil Boyle went over and asked Susan if it was true.

'We're promised to wan another, Phil,' she said frankly. It happened that Jack Doney was coming across towards them, but still Phil could have said something if it was ready on his tongue. As it was, he was silent till Jack came near, then he went away.

That evening Susan told her mother that she was going to marry Sean Friel, but that they didn't want to make it known for sure yet.

'God bless the two of ye,' Mary Manus said, after a short silence. 'I always hoped it'd be Charlie Doogan,' she added: 'I had him marked out for ye since the day he jumped in an' saved ye at the Point. But it's your life that's to be lived, me girl, not mine,' Then she kissed her daughter. But she made an excuse out to the byre, where she cried her fill among the friendly cows.

Charlie and Sally were alone that evening at tea-time, for Charlie was late in coming in.

'I'm thinkin' of goin' to America, Sally,' Charlie said. 'I don't like leavin' you with the whole house on yer shoulders, but I'd like to go. I'm very mixed up somehow. I want to go, Sally.'

'Ye heard about Susan Manus?'

'I did,' he said. 'It's not that.'

'It's that other wan has ye mixed up, Charlie. What does she want hangin' after ye? Sure it's never to come to live on the island she'd do.'

The way the girl went probing for the cause made him uncomfortable. 'I'd want to go anyway, Sally. I didn't see her since I came back, much,' he said.

Sally sighed. 'Maybe,' she said doubtfully.

'I promised me mother to help ye with the childer,' he said.

'We're not that bad now,' Sally said.

Both were silent for some minutes. 'When were ye thinkin' of goin'?' Sally asked.

'I'll go to Scotland first, an' earn me passage. Then I'll slip away from there.'

Sally's eyes were moist. 'I'll be very lonely, Charlie.'

Two of the children came in, and nothing further was said.

Phil Boyle and a few others crossed over to Arranmore to give word of the dance. When Phil came back he was drunk. Drink made a madman of Phil. Word was brought quickly to Charlie Doogan. This time, however, Charlie was the wrong selection. Phil got into a rage when he saw him. He took the lapels of Charlie's coat in his two hands.

'Charlie Doogan,' he roared, 'Charlie Doogan.'

'All right, Phil, all right,' Charlie soothed.

'Charlie Doogan, ye're a bastard. D'ye hear me, ye're a cowardly bastard.'

'Phil, Phil,' Charlie said.

'Phil, Phil, Phil, Phil; ye made a Phil of me. Ye an' yer damned cowardliness.'

'All right, Phil,' Charlie said. 'Get a bit sense, man,' he addes, shaking him a little.

'Sense? Damn ye, Charlie Doogan,' he said, and then suddenly he struck Charlie fair in the mouth with his clenched fist.

Charlie grappled with him. They rocked up against the table and smashed a plate. They fell on the floor together, Phill all the time hammering with his fists.

Phil's mother was crying in panic. His young brothers and sisters were clustered in the kitchen bed. 'Phil, Phil, a mhic,' the mother said, shaking the holy water over him and praying.

'Damn ye, Phil,' Charlie said, his anger rising under the rain of blows. 'What hell's wrong with ye?'

'What hell's wrong with me?' Phil said. 'What hell's wrong with me? Keepin' out of yer way all these years, an' now he steps in.'

'My God, Phil!' Charlie said. 'My God, Phil!' he choked. 'Phil, Phil!' he said again.

Phil relaxed in his grasp. 'Was it me cut yer mouth, Charlie?' Phil asked.

'Get up, Phil, get up like a good boy.'

'I – I – struck ye, Charlie,' Phil said. 'I was mad, Charlie; kick me, Charlie.'

'Sit down the two of ye an' take a mouthful of tay,' Phil's

mother said. Turning to the children, 'Here, run ye away out an' play yerselves,' she said. Then she too went out, pulling the door to after her, and went over to Sally Doogan's.

Neither Phil nor Charlie went to the dance. They sat up until morning, and then went across to the Port. Charlie saw Phil off at the station, and would follow him to Scotland as soon as he had things fixed up about home. Thence they would go to America. Phil was running away, not so much because Susan Manus was now beyond him, but because he didn't realize it when she was not; Charlie wondered whether it was because Ruth was within his reach, rather than beyond it, that he was restless. Ruth couldn't live the life on the island, he told himself.

CHAPTER 42

Sean Friel had come to the dance in uniform. He looked very grand and stiff, and some of the people thought him a little distant. He kept up in the corner with the school teacher and the Arranmore curate's sister when he was not dancing. He danced often with Susan Manus; and the curate's sister talked to Susan a good deal between the dances. But although Friel saw Susan home from the dance, the island was slow to decide that it was to be a match. Charlie had not been present, for one thing; on account of the way Phil Boyle was, Charlie was kept busy. But the matter was discussed at every fireside, and argued over by the boys and girls. There was some feeling against Susan for throwing over an island man for a stranger, especially since the islander was Charlie. That couldn't last, however, for Susan and Charlie were friendly al the time, and were seen joking together earlier on the evening of the dance.

Phil Boyle's going away was another piece of news. Charlie

Doogan had a black eye, and it was one of Susan's wonders that Phil should do such a thing to Charlie. But then Charlie had seen Phil off at the station.

It was a couple of days after the dance before Charlie and Susan met. She was coming down the field after leaving a can of buttermilk in Rosie the Hill's, walking very slowly she was; Charlie thought she looked a bit down-hearted too; perhaps that was why he called across to her.

'A penny for them,' he said.

She came towards him where he leaned on his spade. 'Indeed they're mixed enough, Charlie,' she said.

'It's not mixed they should be, Susan, if what they're sayin' is true.'

'Charlie, suppose ye were after bein' out in the Port, an' the doctor's sister agreed to marry ye, would ye be happy?'

He stuck the spade deep in the ground, and came over to sit on the stone fence. 'Taht's a quare question, Susie,' he said.

'But would ye, Charlie?'

'It would be madness for me to ask her come here on the island, Susie; greater madness to let her.'

'An' supposin' she had a grand place away somewhere, would ye go, Charlie?'

'A man couldn't do that: but it's different for a woman.'

'But what about the island, Charlie: wouldn't a body miss the island?'

'Ye would for a wee while,' he said.

'Oh, I don't know, Charlie; I said I'd marry Sean; I was all tied up with thoughts about him from the first day he came. But the other night at the dance he was all dressed up with ribbons an' braid, an' buttons like a stationmaster. He looked like a thing that couldn't happen on the island. An' then the girls were different to me, an' left me to the priest's sister to talk to me, an' I was frightened. I thought I was losin' everybody, losin' the island. When I came home I cried me heart out in bed, an' didn't sleep a wink.'

'Susie! Susie!' Charlie sympathized, putting an impulsive hand on her arm.

He had heard Susan cry once. It was the night he had gone wild with drink. It was her cry had sobered him.

'Aren't ye fond of him, Susie?'

'I suppose I am, but I'm frightened, somehow. Do ye know what I was thinkin' the other night, Charlie? It's a pity you an' me didn't make strong love to wan another,' she said with sudden energy, her face glowing. 'But ye were different since the stormy day, Charlie. It was her made ye run away to the Lagan.'

'It was, I suppose,' he said. 'I'll be followin' Phil soon. Phil went away sudden I –' Then he stopped.

'Charlie, d'ye know why Phil went away?' she asked.

'Phil was very fond of ye, Susie; an' I never knew. I never thought.'

'God help us all, what a quare world!' she said. 'I wish I could run away too. Charlie, how would I live away in a city? Sean says he's gettin' a great job, an' we'll have motor-cars an' all, and that Collins thinks a lot of him.'

'Are ye fond of him, Susie?'

'Sometimes I wonder, Charlie.'

'Well, make sure of that, Susie,' he said. 'That's the thing to make sure of,' he added.

Then Susan went home. Charlie did a lot of worrying about her and he found himself remembering many things that had passed between them.

CHAPTER 43

There came word to the island that it was to be a good season for kelp. Charlie Doogan and Neil Rodgers decided to give the season to it. They cut big cargoes of seaweed near Island Crone and dried it on the sandbanks. There was a good price for the first lot burned. Charlie was anxious to leave things easy for Sally, and welcomed a summer's work at home. He put in a crane for her instead of the chain down the chimney: he put in a cement floor, the same as they had in Neil Rodgers'. He built a new hen-house, and put a zinc roof on the byre. He would not use any of the money made on the kelp to pay his passage; he would earn the passage-money later in Scotland.

During that time he saw Susan Manus on and off. They met sometimes in Biddy Melly's, and now and then they went home together from there, but they never dallied at the turf-stack now, and they never talked much of Sean Friel.

The first night Charlie came along with Susan, Mary Manus chanced to be outside, and she stole in quietly when they came near. She was sorry to find Susan in at her heels. Mary still hoped that Charlie and Susan would make it up again.

Biddy Melly was the first to notice that letters weren't coming to Susan as regularly as formerly. She commented on it one evening when Susan and Charlie and the others were present. On the way home that evening Susan referred to the fact herself.

'It's true enough for Biddy,' she said, 'I hadn't a letter now this three weeks.'

'I heard in the Port the day that things is a kind of mixed up again, an' maybe he's busy,' Charlie said.

'A body'd never be that busy they couldn't write, Charlie, if their heart was at them: that's what I'm beginnin' to think.'

'People may dream a bit, an' never write to them it's about,' Charlie defended.

'That's true enough, Charlie, before they talk to wan another at all, but once the ice's broken, it's me own opinion, any dream that's not written is not all it should be.'

'Ye shouldn't be puttin' wrong meanin's into things, Susie; maybe it's expectin' every day to come home he is. That'd keep a body from writin', Susie.'

'It would, I suppose,' she agreed.

'What about yerself an' the doctor's sister, Charlie?' she asked, after they had walked in silence for a few minutes. 'She's comin' in to help me with a lagh stran' next week,' he said. 'It'd be fine for her to have a day in the stran' there, where there's a glar, an' she'd up to her waist in the dirt an' wet.'

'That's what's wrong, Charlie; wan woman can't fit into an island; another's afraid she wouldn't fit out of it. D'ye mind when me an' you were out on that stran'? Will ye ever forget the cut of Biddy Melly liftin' creels on Jack Doney that day?' she added hastily. 'A fat person waddlin' in a stran' is the funniest thing ever.'

They joked over things like that on the way home, and parted laughing, but a last remark from Susan recalled Phil Boyle. Then Charlie walked back to tell her Phil had written home that day, and that he was going to America in the autumn.

They weren't laughing when they separated again. Talk like that of old times and of Phil put a touch of pensiveness into the mood of each.

CHAPTER 44

On a day that Charlie Doogan went out to the Port with Neil Rodgers, to arrange for salmon nets, he met Ruth Wilson. The doctor and a strange girl were with her. They went on ahead, while she waited for Charlie to scull the punt over to the slip to join her.

'I didn't think ye were back,' he said as he came up the slip.

'I came back yesterday,' she told him as they shook hands.

The pier was deserted. 'Row me to the flags behind the Point,' she said.

She ran down the steps lightly, and got into the boat. He followed her. She lay back in the stern resting her feet on a taft. The boat glided towards the flags behind the Point. They were warm in the glow of the sun.

Charlie held the boat while she stepped out. She selected a spot and lay on her side on the rocks. Charlie sat near her. Neither of them was in a hurry to speak.

'You're a strange boy, Charlie,' she told him.

He looked at her thoughtfully. 'We're both strange – to one another,' he said.

She nodded. 'I don't know whether I'm in love with you or not, Charlie. When I was away I didn't know. I want to face it.'

'Ruth,' he said, 'we never settled down since the storm.'

'I think I would marry you, Charlie, if you asked me,' she said.

He shook his head. 'You'd never fit in on the island.'

'But we needn't live on the island, need we?'

'Would you care for me if you met me on the mainland?'

She looked at him, and away past him to the islands, and the cottages sparkling in the sun. She hesitated to reply.

'I'm just after seein' two people that ran bang into wan another, an' they more or less excited. Now that the excitement's settlin' down, they're not just as sure of themselves as they were.' He leaned forward to her. 'I walked hours of nights, an' hours, because I kept seein' yer face as ye left me at the gate the night of the regatta, an', Ruth, I wondered an' wondered at things; why I should be thinkin' of ye, knowin' I wouldn't let ye marry me an' face island life. It's not that I was afraid ye'd get tired. I didn't think. I suppose it's just that down under it all me common sense was livin'. Now ye know yerself that ye couldn't go out there an' live day in, day out, year in, year out, with just the weather, an' the island folk around ye.'

'There would be you, Charlie.'

'There'd be me, Ruth,' he agreed.

They were silent again for a few minutes.

'There's a hardness in you, Charlie; maybe as you say, it's not hardness but sense. But I feel you pushing me away from you.'

'No man could push you away, Ruth, unless he was very fond of you.'

She held out an impulsive hand. 'Charlie, I'm glad there are men like you. Is it sitting like this on the rocks makes you great, I wonder?'

'Great?'

He was still holding her hand.

'Aye, great, and I'll never know whether I loved you, Charlie,' she said.

Again they were silent. It was she who got to her feet, and motioned towards the Port. She trailed her fingers in the water as he sculled the boat back, and her eyes never sought his. He handed her out.

'I'm going away, Charlie, for a long holiday. Good-bye, my big, wild man of the sea.'

They were both very pale and stern as they shook hands, and the tears did not come to her eyes until she had turned away.

That evening Charlie delayed among the rocks, and let Neil go home. He sat there for a long time.

The rising tide drove him back and he went up to sit on the rim of the bank. On the way a startled curlew rose up with a scream. It went off into the night, the alarm fading out of the cry until it ended in thin loneliness.

It was a hand on his shoulder brought him to himself. 'Under God, Charlie, what's wrong?'

Susan Manus was standing beside him. 'I was after a duck up that drain to the place of the old stacks,' she explained. 'What under God is wrong with ye?'

'What's wrong with me?' he asked, sitting up straight.

She looked at him, the moon showed up his side face: he kept his eyes averted. 'Ye're just in from the Port,' she said, the concern dying out of her voice. 'It's workin' ye a new way this time,' she said.

"Pon me word, I never tasted a drop this day.'

She saw him full now. He was sober. She was puzzled and relapsed into concern. His face was hard. She wondered why his sitting there had alarmed her. She was sorry now she had spoken.

'I'll have the duck lost if I don't run,' she said, hurrying away from him.

He made no effort to follow her. He saw her disappear into the grey shadows, and he heard the sh – sh – by which she drove the duck homewards.

That night he stayed at home and discussed the future with Sally, while he mended a bow and arrow for Eoin.

'Ye're more like yerself the night than ye were this long time,' Sally said.

'Maybe that's so,' he agreed. But he couldn't tell Sally anything more that night.

And it was then he realized that there was new lightness in his mind, or maybe in his heart.

He wondered what Susan would say before he decided he wouldn't tell her that he and Ruth had talked things into some sense.

CHAPTER 45

Very suddenly life changed for Susan Manus and Charlie Doogan. The postman gave Susan a letter and teased her about it. When he was gone she opened it; it was from Sean Friel.

He wrote her to say he was going to marry some one else,

that he was terribly sorry if it hurt her, but that he knew she would rather he told her.

Susan read the letter under the shelter of the turf-stack. Then she hurried into the kitchen. She pitched the letter into the middle of the fire. She went down to her room and sat on the edge of the bed. She clasped her hands under her knees, a habit she had when going to school of pinning her dress thus, and swinging backward on the edge of the sand-bank, kicking up her heels. And now she suddenly threw herself backwards on her bed, and kicked up her heels. And she laughed, and no one in the room but herself.

She told Charlie that evening. He met her as she was driving up the ducks from the caslagh, an excuse to meet him, she admitted to herself.

'An' ye don't mind, Susie?'

'I do, Charlie, I mind a terrible lot.' She was deadly in earnest and for a moment he was deceived. 'I'd have married him,' she continued, 'an' I would have known it'd be a wrong thing to do. I'd have died of longin' for the island.'

Biddy Melly came along looking for her ducks, and Charlie helped her separate them from Susan's. Then he went on over with Biddy. It was an excuse to get away to absorb the news.

'Isn't he the long time without comin' back to her?' she said.

'Comin' back?' he queried.

'Ach, go on; lettin' on ye don't know. Isn't Mary Manus a changed woman since the last time he was on the island? Wouldn't anyone know she's thinkin' on losin' her only bird. Men thinks women sees nothin'; an' that denyin' a thing changes it. What did Phil Boyle bate ye for yon time?' she shot at him.

'He was drunk, an' he's mad when he drinks.'

Biddy whished the ducks vigorously. 'Ye keep yerselves as

busy hidin' things, as I do spottin' them,' she said back at him.

'Maybe there's somethin' ye haven't spotted yet,' he retorted, suddenly voicing a sudden feeling that now clamoured within himself.

That night Charlie waited among the boats until Susan came out. She wasn't going to Biddy Melly's. He sensed that she wouldn't go to Biddy's that night. The whirl of his own feelings, in the two hours since he had heard the news of Friel's letters, had been similar to the new joy in Susan Manus. Her mother noticed the ready laugh of her, and connected it with the letter, and her daughter's joy pained her. But again she was puzzled. Questions that hovered on her lips she left unasked.

It was just restlessness drew Susan to the door. She didn't see Charlie where he leaned across the side of the fishing boat. In the doorway she was very clear to him. He didn't call her but he straightened up, leaning forward a little towards the open door. And then Susan began to walk slowly down the street, and across towards the boats.

It was a healthy kind of a night, with a warm southern breeze, and a flood-tide, the sea shimmering in a jellied haze. And then suddenly Charlie gurgled, almost growled a laugh, and Susan stood. She saw him across the throbbing haze that was splashed with moonlight, and she staggered towards him, as he came bounding to her across the green bank.

Neither of them saw Mary Manus under the shadow of the byre door, and neither of them saw her hurry back into the kitchen, and neither of them heard her chuckle.

'What kind of a night's it?' Manus asked her, his mind on the day's turf-cutting they were to have on the morrow.

"Tis, then, I never saw a night that pleased me better, Glory be to God,' Mary Manus said, fumbling at her pocket for her snuff-box.

LETTERS FROM THE GREAT BLASKET
Eibhlís Ní Shúilleabháin

This selection of *Letters from the Great Blasket*, for the most part written by Eibhlís Ní Shúilleabháin of the island to George Chambers in London, covers a period of over twenty years. Eibhlís married Seán Ó Criomhthain a son of Tomás Ó Criomhthain, *An tOileanach* (The Islandman). On her marriage she lived in the same house as the Islandman and nursed him during the last years of his life which are described in the letters. Incidentally, the collection includes what must be a unique specimen of the Islandman's writing in English in the form of a letter expressing his goodwill towards Chambers.

Beginning in 1931 when the island was still a place where one might marry and raise a family (if only for certain exile in America) the letters end in 1951 with the author herself in exile on the mainland and 'the old folk of the island scattering to their graves.' By the time Eibhlís left the Blasket in July 1942 the island school had already closed and the three remaining pupils 'left to run wild with the rabbits'.

A fascinating story of a strange and different way of life emerges in these letters as we discover not the island of the summer visitor but one intimately known, loved and feared — and finally abandoned.

FOLKTALES OF THE IRISH COUNTRYSIDE
Kevin Danaher

Nowadays there is a whole generation growing up who cannot remember a time when there was no television; and whose parents cannot remember a time when there was no radio and cinema. It is not, therefore, surprising that many of them wonder what people in country places found to do with their time in the winters of long ago.

People may blink in astonishment when reminded of the fact that the night was too often too short for those past generations of country people, whose own entertainment with singing, music, dancing, cards, indoor games, and storytelling spanned the evenings and into morning light.

Kevin Danaher remembers forty of the stories that enlivened those past days. Some are stories told by members of his own family; others he took down in his own countryside from the last of the traditional storytellers. Included are stories of giants, of ghosts, of wondrous deeds, queer happenings, of the fairies and the great kings of Ireland who had beautiful daughters and many problems.

IN MY FATHER'S TIME
Eamon Kelly

In My Father's Time invites us to a night of storytelling by Ireland's greatest and best loved seachaí, Eamon Kelly. The fascinating stories reveal many aspects of Irish life and character. There are tales of country customs; matchmaking, courting, love; marriage and the dowry system, emigration, American wakes and returned emigrants. The stream of anecdotes never runs dry and the humour sparkles and illuminates the stories.

Nowadays we find it hard to visualise the long dark evenings of times gone by when there was no electric light, radio or television. We find it even harder to realise that such evenings were not long enough for the games, singing, music, dancing and storytelling that went on.

THE TAILOR AND ANSTY
Eric Cross

'Tis a funny state of affairs when you think of it.' It is the
Tailor himself speaking. 'The book is nothing but the fun and
talk and the laughter which has gone on for years around the
fireside....'

The Tailor and Ansty was banned soon after its first
publication in 1942 and was the subject of such bitter
controversy that it may well have influenced the later
relaxation of the censorship law. Certainly it has become a
modern Irish classic, promising to make immortals of the
Tailor and his irrepressible foil, his wife, Ansty, and securing
a niche in Irish letters for their Boswell, Eric Cross.

The Tailor never travelled further than Scotland and yet the
width of the world can hardly contain his wealth of humour
and fantasy. Marriages, inquests, matchmaking, wakes –
everything is here. Let the Tailor round it off with a verse of a
ballad:

> Now all you young maidens,
> Don't listen to me,
> For I will incite you to immoralitee,
> Or innatural vice or in a similar way
> Corrupt or deprave you or lead you astray.